THIS RAMSHACKLE TABERNACLE

To Linda,
 I hope you enjoy these.

THIS RAMSHACKLE TABERNACLE

stories

SAMUEL THOMAS MARTIN

Ancaster 2010

BREAKWATER BOOKS
WWW.BREAKWATERBOOKS.COM

LIBRARY AND ARCHIVES CANADA CATALOGUING IN PUBLICATION
Martin, Samuel Thomas, 1983-
This ramshackle tabernacle : stories / Samuel Thomas Martin.
ISBN 978-1-55081-326-5
1. Title.
PS8626.A7729T55 2010   C813'.6   C2010-902964-X

© 2010 Samuel Thomas Martin
COVER PHOTOGRAPH: Phil Douglis, The Douglis Visual Workshops

ALL RIGHTS RESERVED.

No part of this publication may be reproduced, stored in a retrieval system or transmitted, in any form or by any means, without the prior written consent of the publisher or a licence from The Canadian Copyright Licensing Agency (Access Copyright). For an Access Copyright licence, visit www.accesscopyright.ca or call toll free to 1-800-893-5777.

PRINTED IN CANADA.

We acknowledge the financial support of The Canada Council for the Arts, the Government of Canada through the Canada Book Fund and the Government of Newfoundland and Labrador through the department of Tourism, Culture and Recreation for our publishing activities.

 Canada Council for the Arts   Conseil des Arts du Canada   Canadä    Newfoundland Labrador

[1] Estimates were made using the Environmental Defense Paper Calculator.

for Samantha

listener,

encourager,

light.

"Murk, his vales are darkling."
— JAMES JOYCE, *FINNEGANS WAKE*

*"He shrouded himself in the tent of darkness,
veiling his approach with dark rain clouds."*

— PSALM 18:11

PROLOGUE

In the fall, when a partridge takes flight, the drumming of its wings fills the crimson forest with the pulse of a man about to die. In the bushland of Ontario, near Millbridge, life is a short nesting in a coniferous Eden, before the cracking of underbracken, broken bones, or cedar trees in winter scare us to wing and into the sights of the rifle that is our failure as fathers and people of faith.

But Dan Roblin – the old prophet who dwells in the wrinkled tabernacle of his eighty-five-year-old body – told me, in his small engine shop amidst the skeletons of old Husqvarna chainsaws, that not one bird is shot from the sky that God doesn't know about; so how much more does he know each failed father, each disillusioned daughter, each son shot down?

Dan started me on this trip, this long walk along the back roads of our community – from St. Lola to St. Olga, along the Crossroads to Lemming's Lake and the camp on its far shore, and back down West Coon Lake Road to the Ridge – by taking me for a walk to see old Annie Chizim's cottage and to tell me the story of how he jumped to his death in order to live. It's that story – his story – that pushed me over the edge, into the morass of lives that surround me.

Dan brought me face to face with the *shekinah*, the glory, by having me look my neighbour in the eye.

– Bill Smithwick

13	Cliff Jumping
29	Adrift
45	Shaver
58	Up Out Of The Water
64	Rosary
85	The Hammer
111	Eight-ball
142	Becoming Maria
159	Crafty Old Dragon
168	Roulette
179	The Killing Tree
188	Shekinah

CLIFF JUMPING

Dan's tired-looking leather boots scruff the gravel of the Crossroads as he limps along beside me, up the hill out of St. Olga. I walk beside him quietly, hands deep in my pockets: the air is cool, his silence liquid. There is no awkwardness between us as the summer evening breeze floats past us, like water. As we climb higher I feel myself being led under until the blue sky, darkening with evening, becomes the surface that undulated over me the day Dan held me under water in Lemming's Lake and spoke the words of baptism over me.

Dan baptized me a year ago after a summer Pentecostal camp meeting, even though my priest told me I'd already been baptized as an infant. But I felt that it was something I should do, kind of like coming along with Dan for this walk on the back roads.

As we continue down the road I feel as if I'm floating with his one hand firmly under my back, holding me up, and the other — all five gnarled fingers rooted to my chest — holding me under. Just as I'm about to panic and grab his hand on my chest and struggle for breath I feel his voice like strong arms hoisting me out of the water.

Do you see that little cabin up there?
That one?
Yes. That's where it all started.

1931

Annie Chizim cocks one elbow up on the top of the pot-bellied stove, leans on her one good leg and says, "They'll surrender or die." Plain as the white-frocked Free Methodist she is. No options. No middle of the way. Surrender or die.

"Now, Annie," says Wally Wannamaker over wire-rimmed spectacles, "what do you mean by that?"

"I meant exactly what I said, Wally. Those young lads are gonna surrender or they'll be dead."

"Annie, let's not be rash— "

"Rash? Why not be rash!"

"Now, Annie, there's no need to shout."

"Shout? Somebody's gotta shout. Somebody's gotta be rash! A rash is an itch that won't let you sit still till you've done something. I'm not gonna sit still and watch them boys drink themselves down the drain!"

Wally is sitting next to his wife Betty, mopping his shiny bald forehead, and wondering if "Thou shalt not shout" is one of the ten commandments. "Annie— "

"You 'Annie' me one more time to try to get me to shut up and I'll pin you right to that floor even with this gimp leg! Don't try and calm me down, Wally. I got me a holy fury brewin and I'm gonna spill it all right in the laps of them young lads!"

"Annie, you're gettin undignified here."

"Undignified? You have not seen undignified! I'll become even more undignified than this, Wally Wannamaker. You can stake your boring Brethren bum on that! I'll do whatever it takes to get those boys in. I'll chase them with hot pokers straight out of hell if I need to. But they're coming in."

When Annie Chizim gets a fire lit inside her there's no putting it out. She'll smoke and spark like a roman candle before take-off and then she'll explode in an array of biblically coloured language fired through with red-hot passion. She's a fireball all right. A "Holy Roller," as the other straight-faced Free Methodists say.

Unorthodox.

Odd.

Infuriating.

Stubborn as a pregnant donkey.

But effective. Even Wally Wannamaker has to admit that. When Annie prays, things happen. She's got a tenacity about her that bespeaks boldness. Wally pictures her as a wrestler. He can live with that image. However, it's the mental picture of Annie holding God in a full-nelson, waiting for El-Shaddai to say "Uncle," that Wally just can't swallow. Then again, he doesn't have much of an appetite for miracles.

The beattitude, "Blessed are those who do not see and yet believe," is Wally's creed.

And Wally wants his blessing. The fewer miracles he sees, the more solidified his conservative faith becomes. That's why Annie rubs him wrong, like sandpaper up and down the spine. She lives for miracles. She fights for them. She wrestles God to the ground.

– Bless me!
– Let me go, you crazy old woman!
– Bless me now or I'll break Your holy neck!
– All right! All right. Just let me go.

Wally is sitting next to Betty in their Model T as they bounce and rattle over the washboard road through St. Olga. Wally is driving as crazy as a Brethren-born Methodist can on a Sunday, trying to vent his frustration through the speed of the old Ford while trying not to run over a few stray chickens crossing the road near Rose Carrol's rundown cottage.

"That Annie Chizim!"

"Wally, will you watch the road!" Betty is hanging onto the edge of the seat, face ashen and knuckles whiter than the United minister's collar.

"She really…" Wally scrunches up his face to filter the rush of mental profanity through *redeemed* lips, "makes me mad!" The three punctuated syllables ring with euphemized vehemence.

The car rattles to a stop in front of their house, next to Mieka's General Store.

"That woman has no respect!"

"Wally, it's Annie. She's always been that way."

"Well it's not a woman's place to be outspoken like that."

"Well, maybe not but—"

"And she's always cutting in when the menfolk are trying to say their piece. No respect for God-given order. If she reads that Bible of hers half as much as she claims, she'd have read that it was Adam who was created first. Not Eve!"

Always pointing the finger at Eve, eh? Betty thinks as she starts to stew; but she's never whistled to a boil like Annie. She wishes she could but her lid is screwed on too tight. She's not as witty as Annie, but by Peter and Paul she wishes she was!

Since delivering his biblical bombshell Wally feels much better. He knows he's right. It just irks him that he can never say that to Annie. That woman frustrates him nearly to the point of tears sometimes.

"Blessed are the afflicted, for the Lord will smite their adversaries."

Wally needs whiskey. For medicinal purposes. It helps him forget about his ulcer.

That Annie Chizim!

She was an odd one, that Annie Chizim. Dan says this, his steps slow — meandering, methodical. Wisps of long grey hair pulled back in an eccentric ponytail: odd for an eighty-five-year-old man who had short hair his whole life. Tassels of his buckskin jacket swishing.

How do you mean? I ask, swallowing silence, hearing the scrunch of gravel underfoot.

She had a look about her. Compelling. Like her eyes had

seen something she couldn't just tell you. Dan says this, big hands curled in gentle fists swinging by his sides.
What do you mean?
When she looked you straight in the eyes you felt naked. Like she could see every scar.
That'd be kind of unnerving, eh?
Yes, it was.

1931

Dan is trudging through the snow. Big shoulders burly under a thin jacket worn through at the elbows and frayed around the wrists. His eyes are red and moist. The winter wind stings his eyes and squeezes out salty drops. Small lakes freezing to his stubbled cheeks. A geography of misery.

The obliqueness of snow is a self-portrait. All details blurred by white nothingness. Bottled up tears creating a blizzard inside. Hypothermia of the heart. He needs a bottle of hooch to warm himself up.

He hears the rumble and clink of an old car coming up behind him on the road. He just keeps trudging, figuring it's just one of those church-goers headed home from the synagogue. They won't give him a second glance, let alone a lift. Not where he's headed.

A horn honks and makes him jump like a partridge taking to wing.

"What the hell?"

"Daniel!" It's Annie Chizim, bundled up like a baked potato, sitting behind the wheel of a rusting Model T. She hops down into the ankle-deep snow, leaving the automobile idling, and limps right up to Dan.

She only comes up to his chest but it's *him* who's shaking.

"What the hell did you do that for? You scared the shi– " He reminds himself he's speaking to a woman. "You scared the *livin tar* outta me."

"I intend to scare more 'an that outta you."

"What?"

"Where abouts are you headed, Daniel?"

"Well I was ... uh ... you know ... just headed– "

"Just headed where?"

"Down the road."

"You're gonna catch your death in that sorry excuse for a coat, young man."

Dan can't shake the feeling that he's four years old and being reprimanded for locking Vicky Gunther in the outhouse behind the old school. "Yes 'm."

"Now where're you headed?"

He points dumbly down the road. "That way."

"You tell the truth, Daniel, and shame the devil. Where're you headed?"

"Jimmy Lhicty's."

"Your red eyes told me that much two minutes ago."

He stands there. Dumb. He feels like he's going to cry. And he doesn't know why.

"What that Jimmy Lhicty sells you will kill you quicker than this cold will. It kills you in here first." She jams her bony little finger into his barrel-sized chest.

He bites the inside of his lip until it starts to bleed. He swallows the blood. He won't cry. He's had his jaw broken in a brawl in the lumber camp. But he's never cried.

"You listen to me, Daniel." She grabs hold of his collar and pulls his face down to her level. "There's wine in the Kingdom that you know not of." Her eyes are not angry. They're deep. Like the clear green waters of Little Salmon Lake. Inviting him to jump.

"Wine, Daniel," she whispers close to his face. "Lakes of it."

Annie lets go of Dan's collar, turns, limps back to the Model T, hauls herself up into the idling car and jolts away down the road, leaving Dan to drift away. Like in a dream.

Standing on the edge of a cliff.

— Jump, Daniel! He hears the voice in him strike like a punch in the throat, a gulp of icy winter air snagging.

— I'm scared.

— Jump.

Another punch. He can't swallow.

— I don't know how to swim.

— That's the point, the voice says calmly. Jump!

Standing there in the icy road he recalls the summer day he almost drowned. Gurney and Lyle had paddled out with him to the far end of Little Salmon Lake to jump off the cliffs. They'd left their clothes in the canoe and tied the cedar strip to a tree before scrambling naked to the top of the cliff. Thirty feet. Gurney could say fuck fifteen times on the way down. Least that's what he said. Dan had never been to the cliffs. This was his first time. His first go at her. Gurney jumped first. Swore ten times on the way down. Lyle went next. Flapped his arms like a bird. And hit the water before he could cup himself. Laughter. Groans of pain. Wind. All around Dan's naked body but none in his lungs. It escaped in an inaudible scream as he hit the water. He watched his breath bubble to the surface. A voiceless prayer. Darkness.

"Dan!"

His eyes pop open. Lyle's bug-eyes are hovering over his face. He'd been drowning in his dream, the night after his roadside encounter with Annie Chizim. Lyle must have saved him.

"Dan, get your arse in gear."

"What time is it?" Dan rolls over to sit on the edge of his bunk. The little shack is cold. No point in lighting a fire on Monday mornings because both Lyle and Dan have to leave early for work. Gurney has already left. Lyle is bundled up in his winter jacket with a toque pulled over his ears. He's stamping his boots and blowing white air into red hands.

"A quarter after four."

"Morning?"

"Course it's morning. Why else would I be waking you up?"

"Oh ..." There's a crew of little men running cross-cut saws in Dan's head. All he hears is a buzz. Every word is a shout.

"Too much hooch, eh?"

"None."

"What?"

"Didn't have any."

"Then what the hell's a matter with ya?"

"Don't know."

"Eh?"

"Said, 'I don't know.'"

"Oh. Well, best get your gear together."

"You headed into the camp now?"
"Yup."
"See ya later."
"You gonna be all right?"
"Yeah."
"Sure?"
"Go on. Get outta here."
"All right. See you Saturday night?"
"Yep."
"We're going out to Frisky's with the boys then. You coming?"
"Don't know. We'll see."
"All right."
"See ya."

Lyle slams the door. A tree falls in Dan's head. He hates lumber camps. That's why he got himself fired two weeks ago. Couldn't stand it. So he broke the foreman's nose. However, living without work is hard. Especially this time of year. But Dan didn't have to look too far for work. A hydro crew was working on Highway 7 and they needed a man to screw the conductors into the new poles. Dan was no stranger to spurs so he landed the job no problem. It's just these friggin early mornings he can never get used to.

The curse of working men.

He pulls on a couple of old sweaters, ties his cracked leather workboots, and pulls a toque over his mess of hair. Time for work.

Later that afternoon Dan mounts another hydro pole, leans back on his harness, and begins to climb. His spurs dig into the smooth grain of the pressurized wood as he scrambles up the post, leaving a trail of spike holes. Traces of a woodpecker obsessed with symmetry.

When he reaches the top he pulls two conductors out of his hip sack, reaches out to either end of the cross-piece and then screws them into place. The wiring crew comes behind him but their work is more tedious and Dan is good at what he does. He'll be a mile ahead of them by noon. By the time five o'clock rolls around and the sun begins to set, he'll be on his own along this road to Toronto – the wiring crew lost in the hills behind him. Struggling to keep up.

She told me about the argument she had with God, that very week I was working out along the road. Dan says this blinking, drawing up the recollection. She told Him to be with me and God asked her why. Because I told you to, she said.

She said that? To God?

She could speak to Him that way. Forthright. Demanding. God told her I didn't want Him, and that was true. He was dead to me. Long before it was fashionable. But that didn't stop Annie from sickin the Almighty on my trail. Seems she told Him just where to find me.

1931

Six days and thirty-seven miles. Dan has worked hard this week. He's on his last post for the day. Two conductors left. The sun is setting ahead of him. He shimmies to the top and reaches out to finish his week's work. But he freezes as he looks down the post he's on to the shadow that it casts.

A long black cross stretches out from the base. His own shadow suspended there. Hanging like a dead man. Hearing that voice telling him to jump even as he remembers the emerald waters that closed in over his head that day he almost drowned. Sunk fast. Falling along the mirror face of the cliff. No air left in his lungs to lift him to the surface. Darkness clouding in. Green light fading. Everything going black.

He doesn't feel the bite of the harness into his backside, numb toes stinging. He only hears that insistent voice telling him not to be afraid – telling him to jump.

Plunging him back into that disjointed memory of drowning, where he opens his eyes to see Lyle's pimpled cheek. He puked lake water in his friend's face that day. And breathed deep. Wind filled his empty lungs. Life came back to him.

Dan looks up at the crimson sunset, past the unstrung hydro pole. Splashes of blood illumine the cumulus mountains. He takes a sharp breath, like he did on that shoreline long ago. Late November air enters his lungs. Crisp. Like that first breath after death.

A frosted windowpane frames Dan's burly figure as he trudges in shin-deep snow on his way through St. Olga. It's Sunday morning and Wally Wannamaker is watching him through his living room window.

Where's he headed?

"Wally, what're you looking at?" Betty pokes her head out of the kitchen where she is just putting the roast in the oven. An early morning loaf is cooling on the counter.

"That Daniel Roblin."

"Where do you suppose *he's* headed?"

"No idea. But he's walking pretty sober-like. Odd for one of that lot to be out on a Sunday. And not stumbling around drunker than a Catholic at confession."

"Maybe he's headed to the moonshiner's."

"No. He's headed up the hill."

"Towards Annie's?"

"Yeah."

"Well, we don't really have time to concern ourselves with him."

"No, we don't."

"Think Annie will come to service today?"

"Not likely, after what the minister said to her last week."

"Poor Annie."

"She had it coming. You can only step on the shepherd's toes so many times before he turns you out of the fold."

"I suppose you're right." Biblical language always confuses Betty so she finds it easier just to agree with her husband's allusions.

"As it's written, 'Blessed are the meek *and* the quiet for they shall inherit the earth.'"

Betty wipes the counter and mutters a half-hearted amen.

Dan is standing at Annie's front door. Last night's snow lies still and undisturbed over her driveway. A blanket on a bed that hasn't been slept in. He knocks on the door and then shoves his numb hands deep into his pockets.

Why am I here?

No answer. He knocks again.

Frig it's cold.

Still no response.

Maybe she's not home.

But the car is in the rickety-looking shed beside the cottage.

Where would she be?

He looks through the curtainless windows. He can see into the main room. A few straight-backed wooden chairs. A rocker. A quilt. A pot-bellied stove. There's smoke coming out the chimney so she must have a fire going.

But where would she be?

A foot! Just visible by the doorway to the kitchen.

She must have fallen!

Dan tries the door. It's open. He rushes in. Crosses the living room in two steps and stands over Annie's body sprawled on her kitchen floor. She's alive. She's shaking. Weeping. Face down. Holding onto the table legs with white knuckles. She's muttering something. But Dan doesn't know the words. A foreign prayer. Incomprehensible. Except for his own name that she rolls around in her mouth like a mint, the kind his grandma used to pass him in church to keep him from squirming.

Annie's lying on the floor, whimpering. Like a child.

He takes a step back. Feeling like he's opened the door on a person changing. Exposed someone's nakedness. Seen something he shouldn't have. He walks back to the open door, ready to leave. But he closes it gently and stands there for a moment wondering why he is on *this* side of the door. Not understanding but appreciating the warmth.

Sitting down in one of the wooden chairs, he crosses his hands on his lap and hangs his head. Maybe he'll wait for a bit. Warm himself here. Until she's done.

Time spirals upward. A raven testing its limits. Circling. Awaiting its eucharist of flesh. Dan looks up at the clock on the wall. Two hours pecked away. Tick-tock-tick-tock. Like eyeballs plucked from his sockets. He doesn't see the clock. Blind to what it tells him.

He hears a motion in the kitchen.

Annie comes limping out into the living room.

"How long have you waited?"

"I don't know."

"Sometimes it feels like time flies away on you, eh?"

"Yeah."

Silence.

"I ... uh ... was just— "

"Going to stay for some tea."

"Yes."

He stays until after nightfall when the snow starts to fall fresh outside. Covering the earth in shades of absent colour. Night comes early this time of year. Spilled ink creeping across the canvas. Offsetting the whiteness of new snow. The clarity of an icy, moonlit branch against the obscurity of a darkened forest.

Dan is quiet again, like he's holding his breath, like he's blown out all the air in his lungs and let himself sink to the green algae-covered rock bottom of Little Salmon Lake. Either way he's under; I can tell by the water in his eyes, the way his hands are shaking with the effort of treading in memory. I swallow, wanting to ask him why he went to Annie Chizim's that day, wanting to know what compelled him.

 So why did you go?
 I didn't really have much choice.
 What do you mean?
 I'd already jumped.

ADRIFT

The air smells like an old man's sweaty armpit. The muggy air is thick and hard to breathe, especially with this cold; phlegm rattles in my lungs when I try to take a deep breath. My chest hurts. Every time I breathe it feels as if Jim's heavy hands are pounding my chest. In the silence of the stagnant, swampy, summer air I can almost hear his voice yelling at me – like in the memory where I lie still underneath the waves of unconsciousness, my lungs full of lake water.

In the memory I open my eyes. I'm not breathing. Jim's face is blurry; it's as if I'm trying to look at him under water. His big hands pound my chest. When he does it again I puke lake water all over him and try to bolt upright, but collapse onto my back and gasp for breath. I'm belly-up on the muddy shore of the sucker creek, like a half-dead fish in the bottom of Jim's bass boat. When he sees that I'm breathing, Jim collapses on me, throwing the whole weight of his chest on mine. The sobbing breaths that vibrate his body against mine drum a rhythm for me to follow: I breathe with him as he cries me back to life.

The sobs send me into a coughing fit. My eyes fill with water, and teardrops of sweat trickle down my face as I sit here on the end of Jim's dock: remembering. I wipe my forehead with the back of my hand and then lower the hand until my palm is hovering just above the still water. I lean my head against one of the two big wooden support posts that hold the dock two inches above the mirror surface of the lake. I put my bare feet up against the other post and paddle my right hand in the water, distorting the liquiglass surface and sending ripples out into the dead air.

This is where I wait for Jim every morning of the summer. He's been taking me out fishing since I was ten. I always wait for him here. My parents have never minded me spending my summers with Jim; my mom knew him when she was in high school and he lives just up the road from our house on the lakeshore. Occasionally I've heard my dad ask my mom in her art studio in the basement whether or not Jim is actually my father. But he usually says it in a joking manner. My dad's not much of a fisherman anyways; he's an English teacher at my high school and he prefers to read in the summer. I like reading too, and I read lots of Dad's books. But only when the weather turns too cold to fish. My mom told me once that I was two different people, depending on the time of year. I suppose there is some truth in that. Because it's the end of August and all I can think about is Jim.

His aluminum fishing boat is moored up on the shore, turned on its side, leaning against the trunk of a cedar tree. I wait for him to come down from his cottage up the path;

his cottage is the old manse next to the abandoned Free Methodist church. I wait for him to stagger down the gravel path with his fishing rod and duct-taped tackle box clutched in one giant hand and a thermos of coffee fisted in the other. I wait for him to come and help me turn the boat over and push it out into the water beside the dock so we can load it up with our gear.

I wait but Jim doesn't come.

There is a fog gathering along the shore. It seems to be thickening with the heat: steam rising off boiling water. But the fog is pressing down on the still surface of the lake like a lid. It's a low-hanging cloud creeping along the stones and driftwood that pock the shoreline, as I used to creep along the shore, shin-deep in water, under the drooping hands of the cedars, bent at the waist with a tin bucket in one hand and the other under the water, turning over rocks and looking for crayfish.

The fog wraps itself around me like a coarse woolen sweater on this humid day. As I sit on the end of Jim's dock I feel the knitted weavings of memory itch all along my bare arms and pull snug around my neck. The memories help me to breathe with less pain, warming my chest. I can almost hear him in this recollection: "You cold, Chris?"

"Eh?"

"You're shivering there."

"I'm o-o-kay."

"Here now," Jim says as he sets his fishing pole between his rubber boots and peels off his green knitted sweater. "Put in on." He holds out his old sweater, worn through at the elbows and frayed at the cuffs. It's his fishing sweater for early on in the summer when the mornings are frosty.

I take the sweater from his huge hand and pull it over my head. It hangs off my bony shoulders. It's loose everywhere save around the neck. But it's warm and it smells like Jim. It reeks of fish too but that's Jim's smell: the smell of his boat. It's as if I've put his skin on, as if I'm inside him. But it's so warm.

Too warm.

As I recall eventually peeling the big ratty green sweater off on that long ago morning, I shed one memory for another in which the sun is climbing higher in the August sky and it's hot. The air is dry and a soft breeze is rocking the boat. I look back from the bow where I'm sitting to Jim hunched over in the stern. He's holding his pole in one big hand, slowly reeling the line back into his closed-face Zepco reel. His powerful, sunburnt arms rest on his worn denim jeans. I watch him for a second: his square jaw black with three days' stubble; the leathery skin of his face is etched with squint-lines and wrinkles that make his face look like one of the topographical maps of the area we study in my high school geography class. He shifts in his seat. I think he knows I'm watching him as a kid watches a moose standing still in a stream. He turns his head but doesn't look directly at me; he just glances over my shoulder at a gull taking flight from a dock on the far shore, but I know he's taken me in with his glance because he says: "You can sit on it."

"Eh?"

"The sweater. Use it as a cushion if you want. Sit in a boat long enough and you're bound to get assbititis."

"What's that?"

"A sore ass."

We both chuckle as I spread the sweater out on the seat underneath me. Jim reels in to cast again. I look out at my bobber buoying on the fist-sized waves that rap their knuckles against the aluminum hull of Jim's boat. As he casts his line out we both feel the wind pick up a notch.

Jim reels in, silently glancing at the clouds, unhooks his lure from his line and tosses it in his open tackle box. I begin to reel in my line as Jim grabs the gunnels with both big hands and steps over the centre seat. I'm just stowing away my rod in the bottom of the boat when Jim begins to pull on the oars.

I ask him what's up and he says simply, looking over his shoulder, "Storm's coming."

As Jim rows for his dock across the lake the wind begins to blow harder and the waves begin to slap the metal sides of the boat. Jim's broad shoulders bulge in and then roll back as he pulls on the oars and exhales.

The wind builds as Jim rows and whitecaps batter the nose of the boat as he steers the bow right into the headwind. The wind is stronger now, and the waves are knee-high and crashing over the bow, sloshing my face as I turn to the sudden windstorm. "Where'd it come from?" I yell.

Jim heaves back again on the oars and then shouts over his shoulder to me, "The lake, she can turn ugly quick!"

Jim drives the boat headlong into the shoulders of the waves and I look out over the ugly beauty of the storm: the thrashing waves are dark and shining, and in the distance they look still and textured like the impasto strokes of one of my mom's oil paintings. I'm caught in the midst of the storm's artistry when a huge wave slaps the bow of the boat, jolting me off my seat. I look at Jim and then off to my left and see we're not headed towards Jim's dock.

I go to yell but then I think he must be driving her upwind so we can turn and float in and not get swamped in the trough of the waves.

I sit in the spray of the crashing waves that are trying to bully us away from the shore. Jim's sweater is soaking up the water that's pooling on my seat. Soon the water soaks through my jeans and underwear; it's running over the edge of the seat and the gunnels like a cataract, filling up the bottom of the boat.

I begin bailing the water out with an empty margarine tub Jim keeps as a make-shift bailer. As I'm doing this I look up and see Jim pull and sweep the oars back, pull again. Over and over. I can see droplets of sweat and spray beading up on the skin of his sunburnt neck, where they bleed into each other and run down his strong back, making his grey T-shirt stick to him like a wet sail wrapped around a swaying mast. I look to my own clothes plastered to my bony body, and to my one hand gripping the gunnel with white knuckles while I try feverishly to bail the water out of the boat with my other hand.

I've never been this terrified out on the lake.

Jim's hands are shaking with the sheer effort of pulling on the oars, struggling to propel the boat upwind. I've never seen his bearpaw hands shake before. The veins under the skin of his thick forearms are bulging like gas lines about to burst.

And then he digs his left oar into the churning water and drags it from stern to bow, spinning us sideways into the deep, rolling trough of the waves. He pulls from the right and the bow of the boat turns downwind. I can taste the lake in the air; the scent of her is all around me as I sit here soaking wet – exhilarated.

The wind fills my shirt as it fills my lungs, and wraps up and around my back, belly, bony chest and arms like the cold river water that time I lost my footing while sucker fishing with Jim in the early spring and slipped beneath the current. The cold water *then* shrivelled my pecker to an acorn, but the rushing wind *now* gives me a hard-on.

Jim is steering the boat into the dock when the wind suddenly dies down.

"She comes quick like that, eh. Wind on the lake can be up and down more times in an hour than a new bride's panties." We drift into the dock as Jim chuckles to himself over his crude joke. He grabs one of the big support posts as we float in and guides the boat into shore. I feel the beach sand grind against the metal hull underneath me but I don't jump out of the boat right away. I sit there, my soaking shirt sticking to me. I feel like I've lost something and I wonder if being with a girl for the first time will feel something like this. I've been on the lake lots of times, with Jim and by myself. But I've never felt her have her way with me like she has this day.

Now I know why Jim talks about *her* the way he does.

"You done thinking there, Chris?"

I look up from my lap where I have my hands folded awkwardly over my crotch. Jim is looking over his shoulder at me. I feel like he's caught me jacking off. But his eyes are green as deep forest puddles in spring.

"It's okay," he says.

"Eh?"

"It'll go away eventually."

I sit there silently, suddenly aware that my hands are apparently hiding nothing from Jim's eyes.

"I used to have one for a half hour," he says as he looks past me. Then he turns away and mumbles: "Now she only gives me gooseflesh."

Jim heaves his tackle box and himself up onto the dock and then reaches around and grabs his rod and reel out of the boat. He ties up the bow to a metal ring screw-nailed into the rough-cut cedar planking of the dock. He does the fisherman's knot by making a loop near the base and weaving one loop through the last and making another until he's used up the length of rope and slipped the frayed end through the last loop. It looks like a complicated knot, but all you have to do to untie it is pull the frayed end loose and yank and the whole knot unravels; yet all the fuss and storm the lake can kick up – like today – can't pull that knot loose as long as the frayed end is pulled tight through the last loop.

Jim squats by the metal ring; his fisherman's knot is dangling over the edge of the dock. He sits back on his heels and rests his elbows on his knees, his thick forearms crossed and his big hands hidden, tucked away in his armpits.

His eyes are taking in the blue of the nearly calm lake. Then he glances back over his shoulder, looking right at me with eyes the colour of submerged seaweed.

"Well," he says after a while, "after something like that I'd say this boat'll never sink, eh! Leastways if it does I'm frigged like a fish outta water."

Jim squints against the burning disc of the sun as he looks out over the lake; wrinkles like inked crow's feet mark the skin around his eyes.

I'm sitting in the beached bow of the boat, looking out to the lake, when Jim stands up, picks up his gear and asks me if I'll be keeping the sweater or giving it back. I pull it out from under me. It's soaked, so when I throw it up to him it splashes him in the face.

He sputters a bit, drops his tackle box and rod, and then wrings the old green sweater out over my head.

I cuss at him as fish-scented raindrops fall from the cloud of the old ratty sweater and another memory pours down on me: I'm standing in the rain with the same smell in my nostrils while Jim shows me how to gut a fish.

We're standing in a little clearing in the bush out behind Jim's cottage. The branches of the tall red pine trees reach out over our heads; from the underside they look like hands spread in benediction, stretching south towards the abandoned Free Methodist church because of the prevailing northern wind in winter, but from a distance it looks as if the end of every red pine branch is a hand giving me the finger.

Jim isn't looking at the branched phalanges of the trees. He doesn't see them blessing and cursing with their outstretched hands. Jim's eyes are on the six-pound large-mouth bass he caught earlier in the day just off-shore of the small island at the far end of the lake, near the portage to Lemming's Lake, where my friends Bill and Garret and I sometimes camp out.

The air is thick with the smell of fish. It permeates Jim's

green woolen sweater which hangs heavy and wet on my shoulders. The rain falls lightly but steadily from the grey sky and causes the wet smell of tree rot to rise from the earth and mingle with the strong fish odour that seems woven into each stitch of Jim's sweater.

It's been pissing rain all day and Jim and I are soaked to the skin. But this weather is the best for fishing. I think of the sound of tearing cartilage when I pulled Jim's striped Cotton Cordel lure out of the fish's mouth. Now Jim's sausage-sized finger is hooked through the scarred gills and mouth, holding the fish still while he scrapes the scales off its skin with his jack-knife. Jim runs the blade of the knife sideways up the fish's flank; I can hear the sound of scales being torn away from the fish's body.

Jim presses down on the handle of the knife, set just under the gills, and the blade crunches through the backbone and severs the head from the raw, scaled body.

He picks up the fish head and tosses it at me. I miss catching it and it rolls in the pine needles by my feet.

"Pick it up," he says.

I bend over and pick up the fish head. I look at its eye, blind and limp in its socket, and I hear Jim gutting the body. I feel sorry for the fish and I wonder if it felt any pain as it flopped about in the bottom of the boat.

Jim drops the gutted fish into a tin pail of water by the butchering stump as I turn and hurl the fish head into the bush. I hear Jim crunching through the pine needles. He comes up behind me and lays a slimy hand on my shoulder. "To look a fish in the eye too long is bad luck."

"Oh," I mumble.

I must have a pretty sour face on because Jim says, "Don't worry about it," his heavy arm crooked over my shoulders like a yoke. "I'm just funnin you, Chris."

He looks out into the bush, between the trunks of the trees, towards his cottage, and smiles a half grin. I elbow him in the ribs and laugh as I pull away but his big hand grabs me by the sweater and pulls me back; I trip over his big boot and fall into the muddy pine needles.

Cocking an elbow underneath me, I look up at Jim, the rain spattering my face. He tries to hold a stony stare but he grins, chuckles, and then begins to belly laugh as I try staring him down with my own eyebrows knit together in a funny-looking frown. I only hold it for half a second then we both start laughing.

Once Jim has caught his breath, he stands upright and reaches down to me where I'm still sprawled in the mud. I look up at his big smile filled with coffee-stained teeth and his huge callused hand still stinking of fish, reaching out to help me up, and I think that I've seen this somewhere before. In a painting, maybe. Some image I've seen in one of my mom's art history books from her college years. That big fisherman's hand held out and waiting ...

"Well, you want it or not?"

I snap out of it and grab hold of Jim's hand. He reefs me up out of the mud. I stand in front of him dripping muddy rain water. He looks me up and down and shakes his head, smiling.

"You're muddier than a one-legged dog in a deluge," he says then snorts a laugh, turns and starts walking over to the butchering stump. He wipes the jack-knife on his pants, folds it closed and pockets it, then stoops to pick up the pail with the cleaned bass in it.

As he starts walking down the path through the red pines to his cottage I fall in step behind him. I see that he's looking down at his boots on the path, his big shoulders hunched as he passes under low-hanging branches, and he's still shaking his head a bit as we pass silently through a grove of sumacs.

Red leaves hang limp in the rain, clinging to their branches all around us like sticky teardrops of blood. Jim is always silent among the sumacs, especially when their leaves turn a glowing crimson orange in the fall.

I watch him as he walks slowly in front of me, like he's passing through a sacred grove, one hand holding the pail and the other huge hand turned palm forward and raised a little from his hip, allowing his fingers to brush dangling leaves.

We clear the patch of trees and I think Jim's mind must be elsewhere on serious things, but when we've crossed his yard and mounted the stoop of his cottage he drops the pail by the door, turns and hoists me over his shoulder like a sack of salt for the water softener.

"What the—"

"Don't cry now," Jim says as he carries me down the path towards the lake.

"What're you doing, Jim?" I ask, trying to laugh as Jim steps out on the dock. I go to protest one last time but my words are lost in the rain as I'm tossed like an infant off the end of the dock and into the water. When I sputter to the surface Jim is howling with laughter. His clothes are soaked with rain and are clinging to every muscle of his body. He just laughs and points at me treading water and says, "You're a little wet there, Chris!"

"You're not that dry yourself, you friggin keller!"

"True!" he yells as he looks at his sodden clothes, cups his hands out to catch the rain, and then lifts his bearded face to the grey sky and opens his mouth to drink it in.

I paddle in a bit and find footing on the soft beach sand near the dock. I stand chest deep in water, fully clothed in socks, shoes, jeans, a T-shirt, and Jim's ratty old sweater. I look at him, standing there for a second like an apostle in the rain. Then Jim drops his hands and runs right off the end of the dock with a hollered whoop, a click of his heels, and a huge splash as he hits the water. When he bobs his head out I can see he's just barely standing tip-toed on bottom where I had to swim because it was over my head.

"Hey, toss me a sleeve of that sweater and tow me in!"

There is a flash of panic in his eyes and he strains to keep his beard above water and I wonder why he doesn't just swim in. Then I see his eyes blister with fear and I peel off the soaked sweater and throw it like a rope to him, but when the sweater slaps the water the wet *thack* cuts the memory short and suddenly I'm in the middle of the lake, holding onto the capsized boat with one hand and trying to toss a sleeve of the sweater to Jim, who is thrashing and splashing, trying to swim in the big waves.

The sodden sweater falls a foot and half short of Jim's flailing arms so I yank it in and toss again but it's so waterlogged that his end sinks before he can grab it.

"Just swim, Jim!"

"I can't!"

"You're doing it! Just paddle towards the boat!"

"I can't swim!" he yells and breathes in a mouthful of water that starts him coughing and sputtering while his arms are splashing.

I can't believe it. "Kick!" I yell. "Kick your feet and paddle your arms this way!"

He tries to yell again but he's choking, his head going under.

"Jim!"

His head disappears! In a panic I toss the sweater onto the overturned hull of the boat and push off towards where Jim went under. I can't see him. But his hand grabs my foot and yanks me underwater before I can take a breath. He pulls me down and grabs me in a bear hug like I'm a buoy that can save him and float him to the surface. I try to break free of his grip but he's hugging me too tight and his arms are too strong. I can't struggle anymore. I can't move.

My face is buried in the flowing fabric of Jim's shirt, my nose pressed up against his sternum. I can feel his heart palpitations slow as if he's relaxing or falling asleep. I've stopped struggling against his grip but when I feel it loosen, when I feel his arms begin to go limp around me, I kick away and I see Jim's body disappear into murky darkness as I swim for the surface.

My first breath after surfacing out of that memory is shallow and tastes of phlegmy cowardice. The fluids in my chest rattle, sending me into a coughing fit. I can't breathe. I'm sitting here on the end of Jim's dock in the sweltering heat and suffocating humidity, soaked with sweat and sickening memories, unable to stop hacking and fill my lungs with air.

I lie out belly-up on the dock and try hard just to breathe: to take air into my lungs and let it out, trying to take one simple breath without pain – guilt like shards of mica in my skin. But every gasp hurts and I can't hack the fluid out of my lungs, or the conviction that I could've saved Jim.

Jim isn't here to pound my chest and make me puke it up. He's not here to tell me I'm full of shit and it's not my fault. He isn't coming to save me like that day at the sucker creek he pulled me out of the water before I got sucked downstream and under the highway through the deep-set culvert that poured into the chutes. He isn't coming to help me breathe by guiding my breaths with his sobs.

I wait here for him but he doesn't come.

I lie on my back, on Jim's dock, and cough and gag and try to breathe in the smell of his boat. The humid heat itches my arms and legs, pulling tight around my neck like Jim's ragged woolen sweater. I look up and see the green of the cedars and I recall that green sweater in every memory I have of Jim, knitting the memories together, looping them through one another. But Jim has been yanked out of my life and I'm afraid my memories of him will unravel and pull loose from the solidity of my summers spent here with him, setting me adrift. But then again, Jim told me you have to set a boat adrift if you want to push out and fish new waters. It's just that fishing was who Jim was and it's hard to think of pushing off from shore in the boat without him in the stern or centre seat, rowing us on and steering the way, showing me the secret mysteries of the lake.

I sit up and pull myself to my feet and head over to where the boat is moored up on its side, leaning against the cedar tree. I pull it down, haul the nose over and into the water and then I walk around to the stern and put my shoulder against the back of the boat and heave. The boat slides through the sand and out into the water. I pick up the two oars that were stashed underneath the overturned boat. I crawl in over the stern to the middle seat and lock the oars into place. Then I reach up and use the edge of the dock to push off.

I row out into the fog and stillness of the dead, late summer air. There is silence all around me. The air is still and the lake placid but the stir of my oars in the water and the movement of the boat send ripples out into the dead air, signaling my presence on the lake.

SHAVER

I can smell gasoline. On the muggy summer breeze coming through my window. Mixed with the pine smell of woodchips. Damp sawdust. Mud.

I hear a clink from the shed. Across the yard from the house.

Dad?

I hear another clink.

Shaver starts barking. I can hear footsteps under the eave. Going towards him. Not away. He growls. And barks. There's a thud. Shaver whimpers. Stops barking. I throw back the thin cotton sheet and lie still.

Listening.

There's scuffling outside. Below my window. By the doghouse.

Shaver, I whisper. Sean!

My brother rolls away from me. I stare across the bare-boarded room. My sheet at my ankles. My baggy, hand-me-down gitch wedged too far up my crack. But I don't wanna move.

Sean! I whisper louder.

I hear a *shush* from outside and then shuffling footsteps. Headed away. Across the yard. The smell of gas is stronger now.

Sean!

What? he asks, yawning.

Someone's outside.

What?

Someone. Outside.

What's that smell?

The shed across the yard smells of gas, chainsaw oil and diesel. It's Dad's machine shop. He keeps all his tools there. The shop is dusty. Shops are usually dusty in places. But this dust blankets everything. Cause nothing's been used since the accident: since my dad's brother Frank got his arm stuck under the squared corner of a log and got pulled into the ripsaw at work.

I remember when Dad came home from the mill. His hands and his shirt were bloody. From trying to hold the pieces of his brother together. He'd waited for the ambulance, the medics, to sew Uncle Frank's stomach closed so his intestines would stop falling out on the floor like spaghetti.

I remember he walked past me. Didn't answer when I asked him about the blood on his face, his shirt. Walked right past me, into the shed. And took the blades off the table saw, the jigsaw and the skill saw. Removed the chain from the chainsaw. Took the handsaw down from its nail in the wall. Put them all in his tool trunk. And locked it.

Sean? I asked my brother once when we were using pitchforks to tear apart beaver dams in the creek outlets that flowed out of the swamp behind our house.

Yeah, Wes? Sean asked, sticking his fork into a mess of mud and sticks.

Why'd Mom go?

Too quiet.

Cause of Dad?

Cause of the accident. He said this as he heaved down on the arm of the pitchfork, dislodging a wall of the beaver house and sending it floating down the creek, breaking apart and disintegrating, turning the clear water to mud.

But why'd she—

Sometimes people just gotta take off, he said, almost in a whisper.

We spent the rest of the afternoon working shirtless and silent, getting burned under the summer sun. We picked peeling skin off each other's shoulders for the next three or four days when we were in our room at night. After which we'd lie side by side in the patch of moonlight on the floor between our beds because the floor's the only cool place on hot summer nights. We'd be two inches from each other but never touching. Listening to the night out our window.

I don't know where Sean's taken off to. I got two cans of beans in a pot on the stove. I call for him out the front door.

Supper!

No answer.

The sun has set behind the trees back of the shed. The shadows are long. Longer than John deVries, the Dutchman from down the road who drives us to church on Sundays, ever since Mom left and took the car.

The shadows are long and growing.

Sean!

I hear him. But he's singing. Inside something, someplace. The shed, maybe.

Sean! Supper!

I listen. He heard me cause he stopped. But then I hear him again: words this time.

I'll fly away ol' gory. I'll fly away.

I walk over towards the shed. The door's shut. I can hear Sean inside: When I die hollowlujah by the by, I'll fly away.

I can smell smoke. Not like Dad's tobacco. It's not cigarette smoke. Not Peter Jackson's anyway. Or pipe smoke, cause Uncle Frank smoked a fiddle pipe and I liked the smell of it. Sweet. But this smoke's different. And I don't like it. Kinda like burnt sugar.

Sean?

The singing stops. What?

What're you doin?

I hear him. Shuffling just inside the door. I hear him wrapping plastic.

I pull on the door. But he's got it latched on the inside. I knock twice on the rough-cut planks of the door.

Sean?

Eh? I can hear him unlatching the door. He swings it

open and I jump back to keep from getting hit but the latch cracks against my funny bone.

Ow!

What're you doing standing so close for? You trying to spy on me? Eh?

I look up at him, still rubbing my sore arm. The shed's all smoky behind him. He's tall. Taller than me. And thin. Like a broom handle. The smoke and the dark of the shed make him look even thinner. Like his body's a wire grounding his lightbulb-shaped head to his feet. I kinda grin as I think of that. But he's not smiling. He's older than me, but not by much, so I'm not afraid of him or nothing. He's staring at me. Angry.

What? I ask.

You tryin to spy on me?

No.

What're you doin then?

Tryin to call you. For dinner.

Not hungry.

Oh. I'm about to ask him what he's smoking but then the smell clicks. Marijuana. Dad doesn't want us smoking period. Let alone weed. Sean's in deep shit if Dad smells it on him. But maybe not. Dad doesn't seem to care about anything now.

I ask Sean where he got the weed.

Guy at school.

Where'd you get the money?

Didn't have to pay for it, he says, looking down at his feet, his forehead wrinkled.

How'd you—

Didn't have to pay for it! Just had to ... do him a favour.

Everything is awkward and silent all of a sudden and I don't know why. Sean looks at me. Then over my shoulder. To the house. Sometimes, he says, still looking past me, you just gotta take off somehow.

He walks past me, towards the house, not explaining the comment. I turn and look at him. The slump in his shoulders makes him look like a cracked branch walking. His footsteps are heavy. Like in November when he comes back from running dogs for John deVries during the hunt. His boots all caked with mud.

The gasoline smell's stronger now. Sean cocks himself up on his elbow. Rubs his eyes with his other hand. We both listen. Voices. A couple of them. Can't hear what they're saying. But I can hear them dragging something across the yard.

Sean throws his sheet back.

Who are they? I ask.

I dunno. He reaches down and pulls on his jeans. Zips and buttons them. Then crosses the floor to the open window.

You see them?

No. It's too dark. I think they're off in the bush now.

What about Shaver?

He's not barkin, eh?

I think they clubbed him. I heard them club something.

Sean turns from the window. Looks at me. I don't move. Just stare. Then he walks across our small room. Pulls the door open. Stops. Looks into the corner where our closet is. Steps over, picks up his aluminum baseball bat and walks out of the room and down the stairs.

My bus always gets me home before Sean. I'm splitting firewood by the shed when I hear his bus rumble down the Crossroads, past the swamp that winds out behind our house and stretches back into the woods.

The bus stops. Shaver starts barking because he knows Sean's home. I swing the axe over my shoulder. And heave it down. *Thack*! Into a gnarled chunk of birch. The block of wood doesn't split. The axe head's buried halfway into the dark wood. Water's pussing out around it.

I look up. And see Sean coming down the driveway. Limping.

Sean, what's wrong?

He doesn't answer. Or look up. He just limps towards the house. I run up to him. He glances at me. His one eye's swollen shut. It's puffy and blue. Like an over-ripe plum.

What happened?

Nothin, he says. But I can see blood lines around his teeth. And his bottom lip's swollen. He's bleeding somewhere in his mouth, still.

Who did this? I ask.

The guys.

What guys, Sean?

Silence. He takes a step away. Looks up at the sun. Then drops his eyes to the dirt.

Sean?

They found out I did him a favour.

Did who a favour?

For the weed.

What'd they find out?

They just kept yellin it. Spittin it in my face. Over and over. While they beat the snot outta me. Out behind the school.

Who? What were they yelling?

I jump out of bed. Walk across the plank floor to the window. And look out into the dark. I can hear Sean on the porch under the eave. Then I hear something over in the trees. Behind the shed. There's a flick of a flame. A Zippo, I think.

I still smell gas.

Then a torch is lit. It's a ball of burning cloth that must have been soaked in oil from the shed and knotted on the end of a stick. Looks like one of Dad's spare axe handles. It's in the hand of a boy three times Sean's size. The boy holds the torch up higher. I can see three others. They're all wearing the same jackets. Black, burgundy and yellow. School colours. They're rugby players, I think. I only know Bill Smithwick on the team, but he's not one of the three.

I recognize their faces but I don't know their names. They're from down the road, past St. Olga. Towards Highway 62. They're all standing there. Smirking. Shaver's between two of them. He's soaking wet. And there's an empty gas can on its side in front of him. They got two leashes on him. Pulling him opposite ways. To hold him still and away from them. Looks like they duct-taped his mouth shut so he can't bark. Or bite them.

I see Sean step out from under the eave. Gripping the bat in his right hand.

The boys across the yard see him.

Hey, cocksucker!

Sean hefts the bat so the blunt end's up and pointing at them. His arm's shaking. He doesn't say anything. Just stares across at them.

There's the cocksuckin fag! says one of the three standing by Shaver, not holding a leash. He steps forward, toward where Sean is standing.

We got somethin for ya, fag.

Sean doesn't move.

The guy stops about six feet from him. Faggot, he says as he unzips his pants, Want some? He reaches into his pants and pulls his dick out. He just lets it hang on the outside of his pants. I don't know why. I see Sean's shoulders shaking. I don't know if he's angry or scared.

You want some sausage, cocksucker? The boy takes a step closer.

Sean raises the bat an inch.

Got somethin for you if you do, he says, pulling out a ziplock bag from his jacket pocket. I can't see what's in it. But he holds it up. Sean looks at it.

Just a little blow and it's all yours, faggot. The boy is still standing there, dick hanging out of his pants. One hand on his hip. The other holding the ziplock bag.

Sean doesn't move for the longest time. Then he lowers the end of the bat. Rests it on the ground. Hangs his head.

Is that a yes, you sick faggot? the boy says as he steps up to Sean.

Sean lifts his head.
The guy's only a foot away from him.
Sean stares him in the face.
You that fuckin desperate to get high?
I can barely hear Sean say, No.
Then before I can take a breath Sean swings the bat up over his head. The guy turns to run, grabbing at his dick. Trying to get it back in his pants. But Sean heaves the bat down — like an axe to the splitting block — cracking its full force against the guy's knee.

I hear him yell as his leg bends in with a sickening snap of bone. He collapses. Cursing. Crawling away from Sean who is standing over him. Raising the baseball bat. Getting ready to crack another bone in the guy's body.

Sean grips the bat. Above his head. With both hands. The guy with the torch yells. Drops it. Goes to rush forward but is blown off his feet when the dropped torch ignites the pool of gas Shaver and the other two are standing in.

There's a flash. Like sheet lightning.
And a big ball of flame.
The two holding the leashes drop to the ground, rolling to put out their burning jackets. They fall away from the fire. Letting the leashes go. I see Shaver, fur ablaze, swing his head violently. Trying to snap open his taped jaws.

I can't look away.
I see Sean drop the bat. He yells: Shaver!
The dog hears. Somehow. In the fire. And runs — his fur burning and falling off in clumps — toward my brother. Sean jumps over the guy on the ground with the broken knee.

Shaver! he yells again.

But Shaver stops. Paws at the melting tape around his snout. Drops to the ground and rolls. Trying to put out the flames. But they won't go out.

I can smell burnt fur. Heavy in the air. Like vomit and wood smoke. The smell breaks my freeze. I turn and run to the bedroom door. Down the stairs. And out the front door. To see Sean running to Shaver. Grabbing at Shaver's burning body. Ignoring the clawing and mauling as the tape melts enough for Shaver to snap his jaws at the flames eating his body. And my brother's arms in those flames. Trying to save him.

I go to yell but there are no words in my mouth. Just a scream. As I watch, Sean grabs Shaver's writhing, burning body and lifts the dog. Hefting it. Holding the flames – the burning skin – to his chest. Flames catching his clothes, hair, face on fire as he runs. Runs. Faster than I've ever seen. Flaming. Burning. Like a jet engine roaring to life. Disappearing into the night, behind the house.

All I see is a ball of flame. Running up the granite slope. Towards the swamp.

I see the burning orb – my brother and his dog – fly off the granite edge.

And disappear.

Dad's buzzing my hair for the funeral. This is how we've always had our hair cut. He uses old hand clippers. Kind of like sheep sheers. And clips us almost bald.

But there's no *us* anymore.

Just me.

And Dad.

But it's like Dad is in another room. Ever since he started on sleeping pills a while back. Even when he's standing over me, clipping my hair, it's like he's not there. He hasn't cried. Not since we pulled Sean out of the swamp. His skinny body all mangled. And burnt. His skin falling off like little scraps of soaked paper.

We pulled him out of the swamp in the night. Didn't find Shaver till the next day. His body washed up on a clump of reeds. Already half eaten by crows.

Sean tried, but he didn't save the dog or himself.

But that's the thing, eh?

Nothing would've happened to Sean if he hadn't tried to save Shaver.

Why? I keep asking myself. Why'd he do it?

Shaver was a good dog. But not the brightest. He'd been hit by a car once. Trying to bite at its front tires. He ate his own shit sometimes. And he barked too much.

Shaver would bark whenever Sean got off the bus. But Sean loved him.

He loved that dog as much as he hated our house. Its silence and emptiness since the accident. Dad sitting like a corpse in a chair by the kitchen window. Day after day. Waiting for Uncle Frank to come down the driveway and have a beer with him on the porch, like they used to before the accident – before Mom left. As much as I imagine Sean wanted to take off, still, it was his love for that stupid dog that hijacked that dream.

I'm angry. So angry I want to cry. But I can't. My eyes are dry as sawdust. Staring at the stove. At the fire flickering through the slats of the air vent. I don't know why Dad lit a fire on a summer day. Probably didn't know what else to do.

I hear Dad sweeping up my hair. He dusts it all onto the dustpan. Then he goes over to the stove. Lifts the lid. And throws my hair into the fire.

UP OUT OF THE WATER

When ten-year-old Harold Witaker showed up at Vicky's cottage at 6:30 pm on a Wednesday evening in July, he had a cut just under his eye, which was swollen shut with a deep purple shiner.

"Well, what happened to you, Mister Witaker?" she asked when she opened the screen door of the porch for him. He didn't answer, only smiled at the fact she had called him Mister Witaker, which made him feel, possibly for the first time in his life, important.

"Not interested in talking tonight, eh?" she said as she stood aside and told him to come on in but that Dick was out fishing with Reg from next door. Harold learned how to whittle from Dick, who gave the boy his first jack-knife around the time Harold's Grandpa Earn gave him his battered old violin because the cancer was eating him up and doctors told him he wouldn't last the year.

Harold had brought the violin over to show Dick

what he could play. But after about ten minutes of a scratching and tortured sound that made Dick think of driving slowly over a cat, he said, "Well that's fine, Harold. How about I give you this jack-knife and I teach you how to whittle."

That is why Vicky assumed Harold was there to see Dick, but as the little boy walked through the open screen door he seemed unconcerned about Dick's absence.

His small fingers wrapped in a momentary fist around a corner of Vicky's apron as he passed her by, but he let go without looking up at her — her hair all black and curly despite her being sixty-three and it being unwashed.

Since he hadn't answered her yet and he seemed okay to meander over to the table by the counter that divided the kitchen from the dining room area and plump himself in Dick's chair, she decided not to pester him with questions — for which, though he couldn't articulate the cotton candy flavour in his mouth as gratitude, he looked on her as he had seen his mother look on the statue of the Virgin.

He began to stack the dirty mugs on the table three high. Vicky wondered why in the sam-hill Dick needed a clean mug for every one of his six cups of coffee each day. She watched as Harold reached for the kiln-fired clay mug her daughter Reece had made for Dick for Father's Day back when she was in high school.

"Not that one."

Harold looked up at her as he shot his arm back into his chest. But when he saw there was no fierceness in her eyes his mouth loosened and he grinned as he put the precious mug on the counter and gently pushed it toward her.

"Thank you, Mister Witaker."

He smiled, folded his hands and then sat on them. His swollen eye was to her so she couldn't see what he was looking at through the screen door. She only saw his fidgeting until finally she said, "I feel like going out in the boat. Dick's out in Reg's. You wanna come with me?"

Harold smiled and Vicky could see he was missing a few teeth. You're a rough-tumble kid, aren't you? she thought, but beneath that thought concern snagged at her heart like that hook in her skin that time Dick didn't look where he was casting and caught the back of her neck.

The only lifejacket she had that was even remotely close to Harold's size was about three sizes too big for him. Makes you look like David in Saul's armour, Vicky thought, recalling the story from last Sunday's lesson at the United Church, where she played the organ but didn't listen to most of what the preacher said, except the stories, which she liked. Especially the story of Deborah from Judges, when Jael, a nondescript woman, mustered up enough courage to drive a tent spike clean through the pagan king's skull while he slept – since Barak, the general of Israel's army, was a coward.

One for us women, Vicky thought, imagining herself momentarily as Jael. But the thought of pounding a tent peg though a man's temple made her queasy and a little dizzy so that she had to lean on the oar she was carrying as she walked down their gravel driveway beside Harold.

She was thinking – A chicken I can clean and not think twice about – when Harold pulled on her lifejacket and pointed excitedly out toward the island.

"Yes," she said, barely perceiving the distant aluminum boat. "That's Dick and Reg out there, fishing the rock ledge. We'll row out to them, you and I. You know how to row, do you?"

Harold blinked at her as she stared up at him – her in the boat after a bit of an arthritic struggle and him still standing on the dock. He blinked again but didn't say yes or no to the question.

"Well," Vicky said, reaching out her hand, "tonight you learn, okay?"

Harold took the proffered hand and leapt into the boat, rocking it enough to make Vicky exclaim, "Don't tip us now!"

The boy laughed and sat as unassumingly as a prince – for that's how he felt at that moment – on the centre seat facing Vicky in the stern.

She showed him how to row: how to glance over his shoulder as he pulled on the oars to make sure the boat was pointing true. Once his oar skipped and he almost fell over backwards. When he scrambled back upright he saw Vicky soaking wet from the splash, a few black curls pasted to her forehead. He looked at her wide-eyed, waiting for a rebuke, but when none came and he saw the smirk begin to creep across her lips, he smiled and they both laughed.

When they were about halfway across the lake, Vicky heard the buzz of a motor starting up behind them. She glanced and saw Reg's nephew, Ben LeBou, spinning his uncle's other boat – mounted with a 9.9 Honda motor – to full throttle and skipping the light craft over the glass surface of the lake.

As Harold rowed, she watched Ben fire out toward the beach, veer back toward them, and begin to do circles around them, grinning as he created a whirlpool of waves. Vicky looked to Harold's young face as the boat began to totter on the wavetips and to lunge and plunge between them. "Just stay centered, Harold," Vicky said, "and keep rowing. We're fine. Gotta learn to paddle in the waves. Try not to get stuck in the trough though!"

Eventually Ben tired of the game and buzzed away across the lake and Harold was able to row out of the morass.

The look on his face was pure triumph.

Vicky asked him if he was ready to head back and he thought for a moment and then nodded his head yes, not wanting to seem too eager.

The lake was calm again as they approached the dock. As they drifted in, Vicky grabbed the rope they had discarded when they shoved off. She pulled on the rope still tied to the dock and drew them in. Then she and Harold went to step out at the same time and they tipped the rowboat, both falling into the water between dock and boat.

Vicky looked to Harold to make sure he wasn't scared that she'd yell at him or strike out. But he was staring at her with a huge grin on his face.

Then he scooped his hands in the water and splashed her. You little imp! she thought and she splashed him back. This started a water war that continued until she looked up at Harold's glance over her shoulder and saw Reg and Dick motoring in slowly with Ben and his boat in tow.

"Don't worry, Vicky," Reg said. "He won't be driving this thing again this summer. I seen what he did out there."

"It's fine, Reg. I wanted to teach Mister Witaker here to row against the waves anyhow. It was good practice for him."

"Nice of you to say that, Vicky, but the young lad's got to learn."

Vicky wanted to press Reg to utter what exactly it was Ben had to learn that life wouldn't eventually whip into him. But she held her tongue, as did Dick, who silently stepped out of the boat and walked with his gear up the embankment, away from his disgruntled fishing partner.

Vicky watched as Reg marched his nephew up to his cottage, next door to theirs. Just when they were almost out of sight, where Vicky was sure Reg thought his action would go unnoticed, the older man cuffed his nephew hard on the back of the head and the teen staggered stultified into his uncle's cottage.

Vicky looked back to Harold who was looking away, his swollen eye to her. She reached out to touch Harold's head. He flinched at her touch so that she almost recoiled but found herself pulling the boy into her in the next moment, feeling his tiny fists clenched in the folds of her sodden shirt, him hanging onto her as she hung onto him – not wanting to release him to the world but knowing the hug could last no longer than the half minute that it did.

"I'll get Dick to drive you home," she whispered. "I'll get Dick to drive you home and tell your folks you were with us."

And then they came up out of the water.

ROSARY

The camp bus rumbles into the driveway and skids to a halt by the crooked hydro pole in the dirt parking lot, and I remember how the camp director told me one of my campers, a Goth geared out with fishnet wristbands, a spiked dog collar and safety pin earrings, had just about not been allowed on the bus because she was cussing out the counsellors and telling the junior boys to go to hell.

I'm looking for her as kids scramble out the bus door and head to the field where counsellors are waiting with cabin names and camper roll-call sheets. I see her stringy black hair and bare arms enmeshed in fishnetting. She comes over to where I'm holding up a sign for the canoe trippers.

You the leader, mister? she asks.

Name's Bill. And yes, I'm the leader. Least that's what my paycheque says.

How much you get paid to do this shit?

Crap.

You don't like me saying shit?

No. Well, that too. But I was referring to how much I get paid.

How much?

Crap all.

That sucks.

By now the other campers have found their way across the field to my upheld sign. The girl with safety pins in her ears crosses her arms over her chest. She's big for fifteen. She stands there like a football defensive lineman and stares away at the ground. The black mascara around her eyes makes her look tired. Not scary.

Any of yous ever been on a canoe trip?

The three guys shrug their shoulders, and the two city-born prissy queens from Toronto give me bitchy stares and mutter something about their social workers signing them up for this stupid f-ing program.

First camp rule: No swearing. So, drop the f-bomb out of your vocabulary along with shit, ass, bitch, damn and bastard. That should be the last time you hear those words. Okay?

More shrugs. More stares.

It's not that hard and I'm not a Nazi about it so don't freak out.

When's this fuckin trip start? a fifteen-year-old wigger with his belt buckled at his crotch asks smugly as he thrusts one hand down the front of his pants.

You forget where your pocket is, Meoff? Or should I call you Jack?

What the fu—

That'll be the second time in less than two sentences, so just chill out, man.

The wigger kid, Matt, scowls and then looks away – his hand still down his pants. Soon all the kids are organized in their cabin groups so we are dismissed to pick up the campers' luggage where the bus driver dumped it in a heap in the parking lot.

I watch my campers as they pilfer through the pile of duffel bags, looking for their own belongings. Matt's got his stuff. The Cantonese kid, Zac, can't find his sleeping bag. The other skinny tall guy with a mouth full of braces, Daniel, just has the one bag, which is safety-pinned closed because the zipper is broken. The two prissies, Mira and Mia, from Toronto, each have a duffel the size of a body bag and just as heavy. I help them carry their bags up to their cabin while the boys file off down the trail to theirs. Jaz, the Goth, is on the trail in front of us. I can see the line of a red thong riding too high above the waistline of her torn black jeans. I look down at the trail and concentrate on my footing as we climb the hill to the girls' cabin.

So, how many nights do we have to sleep in this shithole? Jaz asks in the cabin.

Three before the trip and two after.

And during the trip?

We sleep in tents or under the stars.

You serious?

Yeah.

I ain't sleeping under no stars.

Why not?

Probably get raped by a racoon or something.

Yeah, it's probably a good idea. The racoons are a little horny this time of year.

Jaz looks at me dumbly. Just teasin you, I say.

Duh.

I smile inwardly as I close the door behind me, after having told them to come down to supper when the bell rings. It's going to be a good trip. Tough. But good nonetheless.

Think I'll go and touch base with the camp director about Jaz.

The next morning, after breakfast, the director brings up Jaz's file on the office computer and tells me that Jaz was carving herself up in the night, but not really to worry because her social worker said she never cuts too deep – just enough to draw blood. Kind of like picking a scab, in some ways, she says.

When I ask if Jaz will be okay and if anyone knew why she was cutting herself this last time, the director says that she'll be fine and that she was cutting in the night because of rumours that she gave a senior kid on the bus a blow job.

Did she?

Don't think so. Don't worry, she'll be fine.

I know this is a lie but it doesn't stop me wanting to believe it.

Rain snakes down the windowpane above my mattress, which is on the cabin floor. For a moment I smile: thankful I have a solid roof over my head. I'm dry. But I remember this is the first day of the canoe trip. In twelve hours I'll be sleeping in a tent in the rainy interior of Algonquin Park. The smile slides down my face and drips from the corners of my mouth like drool. I roll out of bed and pull on my shorts and grimy camp shirt before tying a green bandana around my forehead and putting my glasses on. I slip out of the cabin without waking the guys, and head down to the waterfront to portage the three red canoes up to the parking lot where they will be loaded onto a canoe trailer when it's time to head out.

The lake is windless yet alive with raindrops.

Before I hoist the first canoe onto my shoulders, I look up through the tangled boughs of a white pine dripping rain onto my upturned face – my glasses – blurring my vision as I shake my head at this unwanted christening.

The group is fairly quiet during the long drive from the camp to Canoe Lake in Algonquin. The Barenaked Ladies hypothesise about having a million dollars on The Moose 97.7 FM, cottage country proud: putting the wattage in your cottage. And I look repeatedly in the rear-view mirror of the camp van at the kids. Jaz stares back at me from the rear seat: dry eyes green like wilted lettuce.

Give up on me, she seems to say through her stare. But I'm stubborn and I stare back my answer through the rear-view mirror.

Canoe Lake passes placid under our canoes as we paddle towards Tom Thomson's totem memorial on the north shore. Zac is in a canoe with Mira and Mia. During our first day of training before the trip, doing canoeing techniques, Mira and Mia were holding their paddles upside down, whereas Zac could solo to the island and back. So, I thought they'd make a good trio. Daniel is paddling in the bow of Matt's canoe. Matt's not nearly the canoeist Zac is but he can steer better than Daniel, and all I have to do is tell him he'll never be able to keep up and he'll paddle like a voyageur. Reverse psychology. And Jaz? She's asleep in the middle of my canoe. She says her shoulder got damaged in football so she can't do too much strenuous work.

Great.

That might have been good to know before bringing her on an eight-day canoe trip in the ribs of the Canadian Shield. I paddle, j-stroke, slip-stroke, back, slip-stroke, c-stroke through the strait between the two islands – Camp Wapomeo off to the left. I think I recall reading once that Mowat Lodge used to stand where the camp cookery does now. That's the last place Tom Thomson was seen alive. Jaz stirs in the front.

What lake we on?

Canoe.

Is this still the first lake?

Yep.

What's that set of buildings? A camp?

Camp Wapomeo. Used to be Mowat Lodge. That's the last place anyone saw Tom Thomson alive.

Thomson who?

He was a painter with The Group of Seven.

The group of who?

Never mind.

But you say that's the last place anyone saw him alive?

Yeah. He drowned right here in this lake. They didn't find his body for six days or something. Should've come up after three but they think whoever murdered him tied a weight around his ankle.

Why do they think that?

Cause when they reeled him in, he had a bird's nest of fish line round his calf and foot.

He was murdered? Jaz sits up and peers over the edge of the canoe.

Yeah. When his friends found his body they couldn't pull him out of the water cause they had to wait for the coroner to come and inspect the corpse. So, they tied his body to a tree root by the shore on that island. They sat up all night hearing his bloated body banging against the rocks while they sat around their campfire.

Serious?

That's what they say.

Jaz sits up in her seat, grabs her paddle and strokes in silence: Tom Thomson's ghost between us.

The rain stopped when we arrived at Canoe Lake and it has held off all the way across Joe Lake, Little Joe Lake and Lost Joe Lake. But as we hop back into our canoes, after dragging them up the rapids at the mouth of Baby Joe Lake, the rain-pregnant clouds' water breaks. Jaz's silence turns to muttered complaining. I try to smile but the rain is cold. I pull my T-shirt off and stuff it inside my lifejacket to keep it dry. I can hear Jaz mumble about the f-ing rain from underneath her rain poncho, which is little more than a glorified garbage bag I snagged from the *Maid of the Mist* boat tour on a weekend trip to Niagara Falls while I was doing my master's at the University of Toronto this past year.

How long is this supposed to last for? Jaz asks.

Eh?

She turns and shouts over her shoulder: You deaf? I said, How long is this rain supposed to keep up?

Don't know. Long enough to get us thoroughly soaked, I imagine.

Shit.

You want to gather the firewood when we get to the site?

Why me?

For swearing.

Thought you said you weren't a Nazi about that.

I'm not. But I'm not deaf either.

Sure about that?

Eh?

Never mind.

Night came early, which was good because I wanted to hit the sack and I needed some time away from Jaz. Six hours in a canoe with her was enough. Thankfully we're in different tents. I feel kind of bad though, because Mira and Mia treat Jaz like a walking lump of leprosy. That could be because Jaz tried to strangle Mia with a length of nylon rope. That was when we first got to the site. When I yelled at her she said she was just showing the girls how to get high. Mira called her an f-ing man-whore and I think that's when I lost it and said if anyone pulled a stunt like that again I'd duct-tape them to a tree, douse them in honey and leave them for the bears. No incidents since, but it's only been a few hours. And since then Mia and Mira have kept away from Jaz. I feel bad about forcing them to share a tent, but I'm not about to mix guys and girls. Bringing home a pregnant fifteen-year-old from a canoe trip can get you fired pretty quickly. That's the rumour, anyhow, about the guy who had the job before me. So not much to do but hit the sack and see what morning brings.

God, hold Jaz's hands tonight so she won't cut herself.

And just to make sure my prayer gets answered I unzip my sleeping bag, crawl out of the tent and take the hatchet and jack-knife from beside the fire pit back to bed with me.

I had a freaky dream last night, Jaz says to me as we both sit by the fire watching our morning breath puff and evaporate in white translucent wisps.

What'd you dream?

I dreamt that we were paddling across Canoe Lake and a hand punched up through the bottom of the canoe. The ghost of that painter guy. And he dragged me through the hole into the lake. When I woke up I wasn't breathing.

Freaky.

Yeah.

The others wake up eventually and we pack away rain-sodden tents. The wind is from the south, but it's still cold, and the waves on Burnt Island Lake are kneecap high. We pile into the same canoes and head for the north shore where the portage to the Otterslides is.

The portaging goes well. That is, after I have a run-in with Jaz because she says she isn't going any farther and I can't f-ing make her. To which I simply reply that I am taking the food pack and heading out with the rest of the gang and she can swim the fifteen kilometres back to Canoe Lake and call a taxi. She tells me I can f-ing well go to hell, but she eventually picks up her pack and follows along.

Zac tries to solo a canoe but ends up crumpled in the fetal position under it when he trips over a root in the middle of the trail. I make two trips: one to solo a canoe, while Matt and Daniel portage their own because I told Matt he and Daniel couldn't do it.

When we arrive on the south shore of Otterslide Lake, a mist gathers, obscuring the far shoreline. I lead the trio of canoes out, but after forty-five minutes we end up back at the portage to Burnt Island. We must've looped around Otterslide Island in the fog.

Jaz drops an f-bomb.

I don't get her in trouble for swearing this time.

Canoe trips, in retrospect, are just a blur of daily cycles: wake up, don orange toque or bandana, unzip tent, slip on wet sandals, gather firewood, build breakfast fire, eat, pack, canoe, portage, canoe, portage, set up camp, build fire, eat, swim if it's warm, go to sleep – day to day. But when I step out of the tent this morning, sunrise of the sixth day, I go up to the empty fire pit and see hundreds of half-burned matches scattered all over the ground.

What the fu—

It looks like someone tried to light a fire using bloodied toilet paper as starter but wasn't able to because of the night wind on the island.

I pull out the tinder kit and the box of 250 Redbird matches. Ten are left. I put these matches in a ziplock bag and pocket it in my shorts along with the emergency Zippo lighter. I look about the camp to see if anyone else is up yet.

Jaz is sitting on the shore in the early morning sun. The black hood of her sweater is pulled over her head. And she has one sleeve rolled up. I can see fresh cuts.

Jaz?

Silence.

Jaz, have you seen anyone else up this morning?

No.

You okay?

Silence. She's usually moody in the morning. Especially when the sun is shining.

You hear anyone around the fire last night?

No.

Somebody used up most of our matches. We only got ten left.

She looks over her shoulder: Do you think it was one of the others?

No, I think it was you and I'm trying to give you a chance to tell the truth, so don't screw around here. I think this but I say, Maybe.

Maybe somebody else on the lake snuck into our campsite and did it like a practical joke.

Nice theory, I think, but we're the only ones camping on this lake.

You think it was me, don't you?

I'm not accusing. I'm just asking.

Everyone's always accusing me of shit like this. She turns away from me, toward the sun rising across the water.

I was just asking.

Silence.

She doesn't talk to me for the rest of the day. She sits silently in the middle of the canoe while I do all the paddling. And she surreptitiously scrapes her fingernails along her scabbed wrists – opening old wounds.

She's talked to everyone else on the trip today, even Daniel. Two days ago she said she wanted to disembowel him with a sharpened stick he was using for stoking the fire. Said he was getting sparks in her eyes.

Daniel has turned out to be the trip pyro: the kid who's never been allowed to play with matches, let alone light, maintain, and cook over a campfire. It's a lost skill among city kids, but on each trip there is usually one who takes to it. I think Jaz is jealous that Daniel can actually get a fire going. That's probably why she rags on him and threatens to yank his braces off his teeth. But, miracle of miracles, she's talking to him today.

However, she won't talk to me. When I ask her at the new campsite on Little Crow Lake, after the four kilometre portage from Hogan Lake, if she wants to help me with dinner – which, for some reason, she usually does – she just walks away and goes down to the water's edge where she starts telling the other kids about her vampire friends. She won't speak to me. But she says everything loud enough for me to hear.

    I have lots of friends who are vampires.
    What do you mean by vampires? Matt asks.
    Like psycho Goths.
    Do they suck blood?
    Oh yeah.
    That's sick.
    Why? Cause it's different?
    No. Cause they're drinking another person's blood.
    I've done it.
    Bull.
    I have.
    You've actually bitten into someone's neck?
    I prefer to have my friends bite mine. It's kinda erotic.
    You're a friggin masochist.
    You have a problem with that? Cause maybe I'll bite your neck in your sleep.
    You're crazy.
    Maybe, yeah. But vampires wouldn't actually do that. Bite someone in their sleep, I mean. We always ask permission and most times we just draw the blood out by syringe and drink it from a cup. Like satanic communion.
    That's messed-up nasty.
    Why? Catholics drink blood.
    No, they don't.
    They believe the wine turns into the blood of Christ.
    What?

They call it transub … transubsomething or other.

Transubstantiation, I call from the fire pit as I stir the package of Thai spice into the boiling pot of rice.

No answer from the beach, but I watch Jaz get up and trudge off into the bush to be alone — to partake of her sacrament.

I sit watching the sun splash orange on the western horizon. I'm on a knoll overlooking our campsite on Little Crow Lake. The knoll is largely barren of trees and vegetation. A couple of years ago a forest fire started on this little hill but was extinguished by the rangers over on Big Crow Lake before it got out of hand. A few spindly white pines still cling to the rocky soil. Their trunks are scorched: black fingers of soot permanently tattooed around them. But when I look up against the pinkish pastel of the evening sky, I can see a few tiny clumps of green. I want to pray. This seems like the perfect place to do it: a burnt-out knoll stubbornly trying to come back to life. But I can't find the right words. I try to say a few Hail Marys, to focus my thoughts, but I remember the vampire talk earlier and all I can think of is an old high school Catholic joke:

Hail Mary Poppins. Superkalafragalistic-transubstantiation.

It got a lot of laughs at school. But it and the silence taste like mouldy coffee grounds in my mouth. Maybe I'll try hard-wiring my prayers directly to the big guy.

God?

A loon howls and I feel an eerie chill creep over my skin like dew as the light fades and the shadows fill up my vision and I stumble in the dark back to the tents.

In the night I hear someone outside the tent, going through the gear pack, searching for something. Matches? Hatchet? What? I listen but the rummaging soon stops. Just go to bed, Jaz, I think as I roll over and readjust my lifejacket as my pillow. I'm just drifting off into unconsciousness when I hear someone outside the tent, crying.

It's been an hour since breakfast: oatmeal with a handful of raisins. I'm sitting by the water, journaling about what I heard last night as two loons float past, barely noticed from the corner of my eye. I hear Jaz's voice behind me.

    Want me to make you a hemp necklace or bracelet or something?
    Yeah, Jaz. Sure.
    Which?
    Necklace.
    How many beads?
    Five.
    Why five?
    Four Hail Marys and one Our Father.
    You Catholic?
    Yeah.
    Oh.

Mary, while you're praying for me, remember Jaz too.

When Jaz asks to borrow my jack-knife I reluctantly give it to her and ask her to stay where I can see her.

    Afraid I'll cut myself?

    It's a good knife.

    You're worried about your knife?

    My grandpa gave it to me. I don't wanna lose it.

    Okay.

    So she sits on the log bench near the fire pit and starts carving a chip of cedar. I watch her over the edge of my journal. Her face is freckled, her eyes green but bloodshot. I smile as I wonder if she's still worried about getting raped by a raccoon. But the word rape gongs in my head, and I look away, angry at myself for thinking, just for a second, that she's beautiful.

    She seems oblivious to my morass of thoughts, however, and she continues to carve the woodchip into a tiny cross, which she ties to the end of my necklace.

    Here.

    Thanks.

    What do you call them things?

    Rosaries.

    What do you use them for?

    It reminds me to pray.

On the last night of the trip we sit around our campfire on a small island at the mouth of Lake Opeongo's north arm. Storm winds whip the flames about. We're all in our sweaters with our hoods pulled over our heads, like a circle of monks, sitting in ceremony. And that's precisely what it is: the last night ceremony.

I pull out a length of thin nylon rope – the same cord Jaz tried to strangle Mia with – so I can burn them all bracelets: little reminders that they've spent eight days in Algonquin's interior and paddled over 110 kilometres.

I measure the rope around Jaz's wrist first.

See if it fits around her neck, Mia says.

We know it fits around yours, Jaz fires back.

If you two don't give it up I'll tie you both together and let yous roll around outside tonight in the mud.

She'd like that, Jaz says.

Shut up! Mia yells.

Mud wrestling! Cool! Matt laughs.

Shut up, Punk-ass!

I'll stab you with a fork.

You think you're so tough.

I stabbed my foster brother in the arm with a fork cause he was chewing too loud in my ear and wouldn't stop. That's why I had to come here, on this trip, while they move my stuff to another home.

This is the most I've heard Matt say all trip, aside from the afternoon on Hogan when he pulled his boxers over his shorts and tucked his T-shirt under his ball cap and ran around the campsite with his arms out like a plane, yelling: wwoooooom!

You stab me with a fork, I'll bite your jugular, Jaz says, staring at Matt across the fire pit.

I'm a friggin blackbelt.

Well, I took kickboxing.

Everyone shut up! I snap as I pull out the Zippo to melt the nylon rope. But the rope is surprisingly resilient to the steady flame. It won't melt. I pull out my jack-knife and cut the small length of rope and try to melt the frayed ends so I can fuse them together around Jaz's scabbed wrist. But the rope just smoulders a little and refuses to stick together.

Sorry guys, I thought this would work. My bad.

Jaz hangs onto the length of rope and toys with it while I stack more wood on the fire and tell them the story of the man whose canoe was swamped somewhere near this island a few years back. The man had been out for a day trip with his two young sons. When the canoe flipped he lost sight of his boys in the whitecaps and they drowned. They say the man still comes here, to this island, each year at about this time in August, to mourn their deaths. They also say that on some mornings when the sun first hits the waters that canoeists have seen apparitions of two young boys staring at them from the shores of this island, silently waiting for their father to come for them.

The fire is nothing but a bed of glowing coals by the time I finish the story.

Thunder rumbles the earth.

A storm is blowing in.

I feel the first drops of rain on my face as I look up to the broiling black sky. We all head to the tents. I look one last time at the primordial darkness above before I duck my head and zip the tent door shut behind me.

The storm pours rain down on our tents in a nocturnal deluge that creates a large puddle under my sleeping bag. I wake up soaked and shivering. Thank God it's the last day. I step out of the tent and it's still raining. So I pull a tarp out of the gear pack and hang it over a branch to make a little shelter in which to cook breakfast. I put a pot of lake water on the little propane camp stove to boil for oatmeal before going to the tents to wake the others up. I stop by the fire pit. Rain is running down the back of my pants, down my crack. I bend over and pick up a short length of nylon rope out of the mud and scattered ashes. Jaz's bracelet. I wipe it off and stuff it in my pocket and then I go and wake up the kids.

 Rain? they say groggily.

 It's raining?

We eat in the rain. Pack in the rain. And begin our paddle down Opeongo in the rain. By the time we enter the narrow butt of the lake we're all thoroughly drenched: even Jaz under her glorified garbage bag. So I suggest to the group that we paddle over to the campsite along the left hand shore by the big rock where a rope swing is tied to a tree leaning out over the lake.

 Sure.
 Yeah.
 Well, okay.
 Hell yeah!
 Whatever.
 I'm down with that, Yo.

Zac swings first and yells out *Sayhumgachan*, which, according to what he told us around the campfire one night, literally means *Death to your family* when translated from

Cantonese, but it's the English equivalent of *Oh shit*! Matt goes next and loses his shorts because they were tied too low around his waist. Daniel's skinny body barely makes a splash. Mira swings right after Mia and both scream like banshees before boob-smacking the water. Jaz makes me go before her. I swing out and click my heels in a Saint Paddy salute before cannon-balling. I surface in seconds and turn to see Jaz gripping the rope. The cuts on her arms are fading or perhaps it's just because I don't have my glasses on. She jumps and swings and screams before splashing into the lake. She laughs and tries to clear her nostrils of the water she inhaled upon impact. I stay in, treading water. Watching them swing, jump and dive in infantile enjoyment of this natural baptism.

The head counsellor, on the last day, asks me how the trip went. I look out the window of the camp office and say, Fine, I guess.

Then the camp director comes in and asks me about the rosary I have tied on as a necklace. I tell her Jaz made it, and she asks about the five beads.

Zac, Matt, Daniel, Mira and Mia.

And Jaz?

She's this knot of nylon rope next to the cross.

The camp director says, Cute, as she walks out, and all I want to do is smash her face through the glass window of the door. I try to erase the thought but it's there — indelible as a line of graffiti on a back alley wall. No one will see the thought, though, so I leave it, thinking of possibly writing it down someday. I rub my hand over the bricked texture of the imagining — feeling its coarse reality, its truth — as I step out of the camp office just in time to see the bus rumble up the hill.

I pull out the hemp necklace Jaz made me.

Look at it.

I run my thumb over each painted bead. I feel helpless because all I can do now is pray. And that doesn't seem like enough. This little craft, this piece of crude camp art, is not as heavy in my hand as I think a talisman should be: light as a handful of dust. But it's a reminder. And that's all I can do — remember — as I watch the bus rumble up over the hill and away. I step out under the steel-grey lid of the sky and start walking towards my cabin. I want to feel relieved that Jaz is gone and that I don't have to worry about her cutting herself anymore. But I do worry. I remember. I can't get her out of my head. It's like she's walking behind me, staring at me. But when I turn, there is no one there.

THE HAMMER

The little one-speaker radio, duct-taped to a post inside the screen window of the camp maintenance shop, is cranked and crackling as Doug grabs the hammer from the sawhorse on the deck and starts pounding a nail savagely through a 2" by 4".

He's got the frame of a picnic table built and he's nailing the tabletop boards to it. His hand clenches the hammer as he swings down, hearing the words, *Hold my hand, I want you to hold my hand*, his father's voice saying the words in his head.

The hammer comes down hard and sparks against the nail.

The woods of the camp around him begin to fade. Green leaves turn brown and black as his anger darkens with evening and his dad's voice becomes louder: It's okay, Doug. It's okay to do this. And he feels his dad's big, carpenter-callused hand grip his wrist, pulling his hand down towards the crotch of his pants.

No! No! NO! Doug yells in his head.

It's good you're going to camp, his dad told him, then maybe that'll be the end of ... well, our little problem.

It's not *our* fucking problem, Dad! Doug mutters as he pounds another nail, each stroke coming down harder, the song crescendoing as he yells silently to a forest of tree trunks, soot-black with shadows.

Sunlight fades with the song.

And Doug hurls the hammer into the dark.

Get a little carried away with the hammer? Krysta asks, running her hand over the battered surface of the one 2" by 4".

Had a problem gettin the nail in, Doug says as he disappears into the maintenance shed.

Krysta looks at the other three boards nailed into place: each surface smooth, each nail driven home perfectly, some through big knots in the wood. She looks up from the table to the dark of the doorway: Doug?

Yeah? he calls from inside, over by the far wall.

What're you looking for?

The hammer.

You lose it?

Guess so, he says, coming out of the shed and squinting against the forest-filtered sunlight shining on his bushy head of brown curls.

When's your hour off today?

Krysta, I work maintenance, I can take whatever hour off I want.

Oh yeah, you're not like us lowly counsellors, running programs and stuff, eh?

Nope. Been there, done that, and they give me this T-shirt for it, Doug says as he pulls out the bottom of his faded green T-shirt from last year, with the yellow camp logo in the middle of his chest; the shirt is speckled with white paint and burgundy woodstain.

Nice, says Krysta as she turns and steps down from the porch onto the trail that winds up from the cookery, past the senior boys' cabins and out to Lone Pine – where everyone goes for evening campfires. Well, my hour's at two. You want to do something?

You like to fish?

Sure.

See you down at the docks at two, then.

Okay, Krysta says as she turns and walks away down the trail towards the cookery. The bell starts ringing for lunch.

Doug's eyes follow her down the path. She's wearing short jean shorts and a bright orange T-shirt that hugs her love handles a bit. Her hair is tied in a loose ponytail at the nape of her neck. And she's wearing flip-flops that clap against her heels as she walks.

She glances back over her shoulder at Doug, who drops his head and pretends to look for the missing hammer.

Doug's listening to Creed on the Moose 97.7 FM, the old staticky radio screaming. Doug lets out a purposefully slow breath as he holds another nail in place and reaches for his new hammer, made from a rusted old head he'd found in a

Folger's coffee can and a foot-long length of wood sawed from a road hockey stick.

He pounds at the nail, driving it home with one heavy swing.

Doug pulls another nail out from between his lips and holds it in place along the chalkline he's snapped. He can feel the sun hot on his shoulders; he imagines himself as an ant under a magnifying glass.

Doug pounds the nail into place, puts the hammer down, spits the nails out on the finished tabletop, and looks down at his shoes: ratty old, paint-splattered Nikes. His laces are undone and splay out on either side of his shoes like the roots of twin denim-barked tree trunks. His dad never let him leave the house without doing up his shoelaces: everything had to appear perfect to everyone else. He imagines the laces sinking, growing through the boards of the deck and into the earth. My roots, he thinks as he looks down, then lifts a foot. The laces hang limp in the air.

Some roots, eh?

Doug looks at his watch: 2:10 pm. He cocks his head, feeling that he's supposed to be somewhere. Am I ...

Shoot! he spits as he turns, jumps off the deck and runs over to the fuel shed. Krysta's going to be waiting! he thinks as he pulls his keys out of his pocket, looking for the little copper one. He pops the lock, wiggles it loose, pulls the door open, and grabs the mixed-gas container – spilling some gas on his pant leg.

Motherfu–

He curses as he slams the door shut, locks it, and starts running down the trail, red gas can in his left hand, fuel leaking out the back air spout as he kicks up dust on the path.

Krysta is sitting on the barge, which is tethered to the end of the main dock. She's sitting in one of the two Muskoka chairs onboard, looking up the tiered staircase that connects the path from the cookery to the waterfront.

Krysta is one of the lifeguards but it's her hour off. And she's waiting for Doug, wondering where he is as she reclines in the chair, crossing her legs and wiggling her toes in her flip-flops.

She looks up the stairs again to see Doug clambering down them, gas can in hand.

She smiles just as he looks up at her.

When he reaches the bottom of the stairs he jogs along the dock to the barge, where Krysta is undoing the front line from the dock, standing under the lifeguard tower.

Forgot fishin poles, he says.

That's okay. We can just go out on the barge for a while.

Sure, Doug says as he unscrews the gas cap of the old Evinrude motor and begins filling it. As he's pouring he looks over at Krysta who is standing upright, fiddling with the knot.

It's a fisherman's knot, eh? he says to her.

I know, she says, not looking up, her tongue licking the corner of her mouth. But some nincompoop did it backwards and I got to pull each loop loose.

Oh, Doug says, glancing back at his pouring job. He cusses when he sees the top of the motor slick with fuel and the rainbow colours of gas-on-water rippling out from the prop. For cryin out loud!

What? Krysta asks, having loosed the front line from the dock.

Ahh ... nothing, Doug says as he steps over to obstruct Krysta's view.

But Krysta strides down to the end of the dock to undo the stern-end knot and sees the gas spill rippling out from the motor over the surface of the water. She looks up at Doug, who is still bent over, cheeks red, trying steadily to pour the rest of the can *into* the motor.

Having trouble, Doug?

His ears start to burn and he says maybe as he tilts the can a bit higher to drain it. He finishes pouring out the can, which only fills the motor to three-quarters, then sets it down and looks up at Krysta, who has pulled the last knot loose and is holding the rope, smiling at him.

Ready to go? he asks, his face sunburnt red in embarrassment.

Yup, she says as she tosses the rope to him, leans against the railing of the barge, pushes out from the dock, and jumps on as the barge begins to float away.

Doug pull-starts the motor, eases the choke in, and then throttles it, cranking the handle towards the shoreline and slowly swinging the front end of the barge out towards the island in the middle of the lake. He watches Krysta as she goes to the front of the barge, swings underneath the railing and stands on the right-hand pontoon, leaning back against the corner post.

He rounds the island and takes the barge out of sight of the camp. Just as the camp dock disappears from view behind the treed point of the island, the handle of the motor begins to shake violently, vibrating Doug's whole arm. He lets go for a second and turns just in time to see the motor wiggle loose of the metal lip it was fastened to, and fall off the back of the barge, into the water.

He jerks his head around to look at Krysta, who turned when the motor cut out. They both look back to see bubbles glubbing to the surface about five feet off the back of the barge, where the motor sunk.

Shit! Doug yells.

Krysta doesn't say anything. She just stares at Doug, who buries his curly head in his hands, pulls at his hair and growls at himself. She watches as he hoists himself up from his seat on the milk crate at the stern and slaps the open palms of both hands down on the railing.

Fuck!

She watches him grip the railing with both hands until his knuckles go white and he pushes himself back, winds up and kicks the back right corner post as hard as he can. She stares at him as he limps about, swearing, yelling, growling ... and crying.

In the middle of his rampage Doug remembers Krysta; he stops suddenly and looks up at her. She's still standing out on the pontoon. He can tell by her eyes – like a child that's been slapped – that he's scared her. There's a cold tightness in his chest. He turns and looks back to where the motor sunk. He runs his hand through his hair in frustration. He's angry at himself for not tightening the bolts that held the motor in place, for not hanging onto the motor. For losing it. And he's pissed because he thinks he's probably blown his chance with Krysta. He let the anger get outside of him, where he's kept it caged up for so long.

I'm sorry, he mutters.

What? Krysta asks, trying to swallow the fear prickling her mouth like a thistle.

He turns to her. I'm sorry, he says.

What happened?

The motor fell off.

No, to you?

He looks down at his undone laces, suddenly embarrassed by their frayed ends and the fact that he hasn't tied them up since coming to camp this summer.

Doug?

He looks up at her. He can read the question in her eyes. But he's not sure if he can answer her. He turns and faces the stern, looking out to the far shoreline, treed with jack pines and scrub brush. There's a dead tree sticking out from the granite shore into the water, its branched head beneath the surface.

As he looks at the tree he feels the muscles in his neck tighten. Like his dad's hand on his neck, pushing his face down. He can't breathe. His shoulders start to shake. And he drops to his knees, closes his eyes, trying to stop the tears with his fists.

Krysta, behind him, ducks under the railing and steps onto the wooden floor of the barge. She slowly walks up to him and stands an arm's length from his shoulder. Part of her is scared he'll strike out if she tries to touch him. But a bigger part of her feels she needs to touch him, to fill that hollow between his shoulders with her hand.

As she does this she can feel his skin tighten under her

touch. But he doesn't move. She feels like she's in a tableau on a floating stage. She lifts the palm of her hand from his shirt, bringing her fingers together and then sliding them out again, resting her hand flat against his back.

Doug feels the hairs on his neck stand on end. He can feel her thumb rubbing back and forth along the ridge of his shoulder blade.

He lies a bit in the telling. Says his dad beats up on him sometimes when he's drunk. But his dad doesn't drink. Never has. But that lie will damage his dad's name less than the truth. Why he cares about his dad's good name he doesn't know, but he does. Anyhow, Krysta will never meet his dad. Not yet. Maybe someday. But until then, the lie will do, seeing as how it isn't that far off the truth.

I got a bad temper, he says. That's why they gave me the maintenance job instead of a counsellor position. So I wouldn't lose my temper with the kids.

Do they know about your father?

No. Just that I got a short fuse.

Ever think of telling anyone?

Nope.

Ever think that might be more damaging than letting it out once in a while?

I let off steam now and then.

How?

A scene of himself jerking off on his cot in the maintenance shed flashes through his mind. He goes a little red, looks down and says: I build stuff when I'm angry.

Like the picnic table?

Yeah. They need one for out in the field, by the fire pit, anyways.

Was that what was with those dents in the one board this morning?

Dents?

When I asked you about going crazy with the hammer?

He looks up at her, remembering how he had hurled the hammer into the forest the evening before. Got a little carried away on that one, eh? he says.

Looked that way.

He glances out towards the island that's off the starboard side of the barge. They've been drifting since the motor fell off. Drifting and talking. Sitting together in the centre of the barge with their knees drawn up under their chins, their arms wrapped around their legs. The camp will be coming into view soon. He looks at his watch; Krysta is past her hour, but it is siesta-time at three, so really, according to her, she has two hours.

Three-eighteen, he says.

We're going to have to swim the barge back, eh?

Yeah. Then I have to fess up to losing the motor.

It was an accident.

Try telling them that. When you got a reputation like me the head counsellors aren't usually that sympathetic. Especially when you keep losing camp stuff on them.

What else did you lose?

Spilt half a tank of gas.

Anything else?

The hammer.

You tell them about that yet?
No.

The swim back isn't bad, a little long – especially hauling the barge behind them – but they make it back to the main dock a few minutes before 4 pm. Krysta hauls herself out of the water, turns and gives Doug a hand out. He tells her he'll tie the barge off and she says, Thanks. So I'll see you tonight at the campfire, right?

Maybe.

Hope so, she says as she turns, walks to the end of the dock, climbs the tiered staircase and disappears down the path.

Doug ties up the barge, carefully so as to make sure he doesn't screw up the fisherman's knot this time, and then grabs the empty gas can and heads up the stairs, down the path and back to the maintenance shed, where he strips off his wet clothes and wanders around for a while feeling free. But that feeling darkens as he thinks of his dad. He takes a black magic marker from a tin on the workbench and scrawls a caricature of his dad on the wall near his bed to get his dad out of his mind: to face him somehow. But he can't face him even in this cartooned form so he thinks about Krysta and tries to extricate what he begins doing to himself from what his dad has forced him to do since he was seven – all this while leaning against the wall, the back of his head resting on his dad's face, the smell of the marker suddenly soothing after the tension snaps.

After he's wiped the floor with paper towel, gotten dressed, and hung his wet clothes out to dry on the clothesline,

Doug heads off for a walk in the bush before supper.

He walks along the path that leads out past the junior boys' cabins, along the shoreline, and connects with the main path to Lone Pine. He keeps his eyes on the trail so he doesn't trip over any spruce roots. His laces are tied for the first time this summer.

He's whistling to himself and he doesn't hear a boy snap a picture of him with a digital camera; he doesn't even hear the boy begin to follow him down the path, away from the cabins and into the forest.

Halfway to Lone Pine, Doug breaks off the trail and heads into the woods. The trees are pretty much all hardwood here and rise up above him so high that he has to stop and crane his neck back to see where their branches interlock and their leaves thatch together to block the afternoon sunlight.

He feels like he wants to run or break something. He crunches through leaves and under-bracken until he finds an old dead stick as thick as a baseball bat. He picks it up, twists his hands around it like he's stepping up to the plate, and then smashes it against the trunk of a tree, cracking it in half and sending the top end spinning off into the bush. He looks up and around himself: searching the forest for a dead tree.

He walks on until he finds one that's not too big – small enough that he can wrap his arms all the way around its base. He looks at the barkless trunk snaked with termite trails and riddled with woodpecker holes. It'll topple easy, he thinks as he puts his hands flat against the trunk that's slippery with tree rot and slug snot. But he doesn't care about the slick feel of the tree, its goo squishing between his fingers as he begins to push against it, gritting his teeth.

The boy who has followed him is crouching behind a bush to the left of where Doug is trying to fell the rotten old tree; the kid's trying to get his camera to focus. Doug doesn't see him; he's pouring all of himself into toppling the tree, forcing its decayed roots to rip out of the ground so its branched head will crash against the forest floor. As he heaves and strains, his arms tremble with the effort and his face begins to go red as the veins in his neck bulge out. He heaves against the trunk, imagining himself throwing his shoulder into his dad's stomach and driving the old man through a gyproc wall the next time he tries to touch him — a thought he never would have had before coming to camp last summer. He pushes and strains, pouring all his anger into the effort but the tree doesn't budge in the direction he's pushing.

He rounds the trunk till he's facing the bush where the boy is hiding and playing with his zoom, watching Doug through the lens of his camera as Doug begins to heave against the trunk of the tree again, but this time the roots begin to pull loose of the earth as the tree groans and begins falling — crashing down.

Doug looks up just in time to see the boy scramble out of the bush and roll away as the dead tree smashes down on the place he'd been hiding.

The boy jumps to his feet, leaves in his hair, his face dirty, eyes wide. He stares at Doug staring back at him. I could've killed him, Doug thinks. Relief pours in on his feelings of shock like vinegar on soda: causes anger to froth up in him.

What the hell are you doing out here!

The boy doesn't answer, only continues to stare at Doug as he pockets his camera. The boy's silence makes Doug more livid.

What're you doing just staring at me for, eh? Go on! he barks. Get out of here!

The boy stands frozen, eyes wide.

Doug marches up to him and grabs the collar of the boy's shirt in his fists, bringing the camper's face to his. Get back to your cabin NOW! he shouts in the kid's face and then throws him to the ground. The boy scrambles to his feet and runs off towards the path, throwing scared and confused glances over his shoulder as he trips through the bush and disappears from sight. By the time the boy reaches the path he's got over his fear and stomps angrily – though still a little shaken from the run-in – back to his cabin.

Back in the forest Doug crouches down and hugs his knees, feeling like all the trees are leaning over him, reaching out branched hands: watching. He rocks back and forth till he hears a crow crack the silence with its caw.

The next day splits open at 5:30 am like a cracked skull; Doug is sitting in a Muskoka chair out on the barge – where he has sat up all night – watching the sun rise and bleed into the cotton swab clouds. His head is resting in his hand: his elbow propped up on the arm of the chair.

He hasn't slept and his hair is wet with dew. He sits there until the light cauterizes into an infected yellow and he hears the bell ring for morning watch.

6:10 am.

He gets up stiffly out of the chair, steps onto the dock,

and limps tiredly to the staircase. He hates morning watch — the little devotional time before breakfast — but he goes every morning so he'll be the first in line for coffee when the breakfast bell goes.

He trudges over to the far side of the cookery where campers are gathering around an empty fire pit. One of the girl counsellors is sitting on a picnic table, her back to the lake, facing the gathering of campers, most of whom are still yawning and wiping sleep out of their eyes.

Give us the verse for the day and say a quick prayer so I can get to my coffee, Doug thinks as he leans against the wall of the cookery, outside the ring of gathered campers. The counsellor on the picnic table waits a few more minutes and then opens the Bible on her lap and reads from Ecclesiastes, chapter three.

There is a time for everything, she begins and Doug rolls his eyes. *A time to be born and a time to die, a time to plant and a time to harvest ...*

Doug zones out the girl's tired voice. He looks over and sees Krysta across the lake of sleepy-eyed campers. She looks from the girl leading the devotions over to Doug. She smiles and he grins back. One of Krysta's campers tugs at her sleeve and she drops her gaze. Doug looks down at his shoes, laces undone and muddy from the walk up from the waterfront.

The girl is still going on: *A time to break down, and a time to build up ...*

I'm always building shit, Doug thinks. I try tearing one thing down and I nearly kill a kid.

... a time to cast away stones, and a time to gather stones together; a time to keep silent, and a time to speak; a time to love, and a time to hate ...

I hate standing here like this, he thinks as the girl concludes her reading, says a short prayer and dismisses the kids for breakfast. As soon as the kids start moving, Doug turns and strides around the corner of the cookery, smelling pancakes through the kitchen windows. He walks into the dining room, grabs a mug off the dish counter, and goes over to the coffee percolator.

The aroma of the coffee is like incense to him; he takes the mug in his right hand and waves it in a small cross, mimicking his priest back home, careful so as not to spill it. And he says, holding the cup to lips for his first sip, In the name of the father, son, and holy haunted one.

He takes a sip and clucks his tongue, eyes brightening.

Doug is staining the picnic table later that morning with a deep red deck stain. He plops the brush into the half-filled can, swishes it around, and slaps it up onto the wooden surface of the table, dripping stain all over the deck, splattering his shoes and his bare legs. He's staring emptily at his work, barely aware of what he's doing.

The radio is on.

The announcer is just finishing the weather report: And this afternoon it'll be cloudy with a chance of evening showers. This has been your most accurate cottage country weather, twice an hour on 97.7 The Moose FM. And now for a new number by Bruce Springsteen: the title track from his album *Devils and Dust*.

Doug slops on another brush-full of stain, swiping it back and forth – not caring that it's bubbling up on him – listening to the pulse of the guitar on the crackling radio.

He's trying not to think of how angry the camp director got when he told her that he'd misplaced a hammer and lost the motor off the barge. The missing hammer didn't seem really to bother her – she just nodded and raised her eyebrows – but when he told her he'd lost the motor she sparked-off. Doug apologized but got a verbal slap with: Apologies don't pay for new motors! After saying this, the director started in on a long rant about responsibility and how the camp was giving Doug a second chance this summer; he'd been sent home last year for flipping out on a senior boy who'd shit in the shower because he knew Doug was on janitorial duty. Doug sat in the plastic chair across the desk from the director, in the camp office, afraid that he'd be sent home again ... to face his dad.

But the director didn't send him home; she told him this was his last chance, though. And she sent him out, back to the maintenance shed to finish staining the picnic table for the sports field, by the fire pit. So that's what he's doing now: trying not to think, trying to focus on his work.

The dark red stain seems to him to blacken the wood that had been a light white pine colour. He keeps smearing the stain over the light surfaces of the table, darkening the wood and sealing it against rain and rot. The more he paints to forget, to cover over his anger, the more he remembers and the more his unsanded anger causes his effort at forgetting to froth.

He slaps on the last bit of stain and stands back to look at the picnic table. Its rough, unsanded surfaces are covered with reddish bubbles; some sections are almost black with stain laid on too thickly, coagulating in the sun, while other areas are barely covered, the stain almost translucent, showing the grainy veins of the wood. It looks as if the table has been used as a butchering slab in a slaughterhouse.

The overcast sky is a grey blanket pulled up over the dead face of the lake when he goes out canoeing with Krysta that afternoon. They happen upon an Old Order Mennonite couple fishing in a small bay. Krysta tells Doug that the Mennonites live on a communal farm across from the camp.

She's silent for a bit as they drift in closer. Then she suddenly suggests mooning the old conservative couple.

On Krysta's count they stand up and go to drop their pants but the canoe flips.

The old woman laughs as her husband rows their boat out of the bay, leaving Krysta and Doug to right the canoe and haul themselves out of the weedy water. Once they're in the canoe, laughing, Krysta asks Doug if he wants to meet her that night, behind the girls' washroom.

After curfew and lights out.

He doesn't take a flashlight with him as he steps out of the maintenance shed, even though the night is moonless and all the stars are hidden behind the black lid of an overcast sky. He stands on the porch of the maintenance shed by the door, reaches inside and turns off the light, and the darkness' heavy lid slams silently shut, locking him into the night's crypt.

He steps slowly, allowing his eyes to adjust to the darkness, imagining the layout of the camp in his head. Soon he is able to see a little and he finds the path that cuts through the woods to the playing field and the girls' washroom.

When he gets to the fence he calls out in a hoarse whisper: Krysta?

Over here, she says, from a few fence posts away. Doug can barely see her.

No stars tonight, eh? he says.

I see that.

So?

So what? Come on, she says as she starts out into the old horse field, walking through waist-high grass. Doug follows her, putting his hands out beside him and feeling the grass tickling his palms as he walks.

They are headed in the direction of the Old Barn. Doug's been there in daylight but tonight he can't make out where the decrepit building stands, crouched like an architectural hunchback against the far tree line. He's walking along, trying to make out where in the field they are, thinking his eyes are closed, when he feels Krysta stop him, her hand on his wrist. He can't see her but he feels her body press against his, her fingers running up the front of his shirt. He can feel her breath hot on his neck as she cups her hands behind his ears, running her fingers into his curly hair, pulling his face to hers.

They press their lips together. Their teeth click. Her tongue is in his mouth; her hands on the back of his head, his hands on her ears. She presses her hips against him. His cock's too hard in his pants. But he drops his hands from her head to her waist, pulling her into him more, until it almost hurts.

She pulls him down to his knees and onto her as she lies out in the long grass, spreading her legs to let him press against her. He puts a fisted hand down on either side of her head, his knuckles digging into the dirt, arms straight, holding his chest just above hers.

Their breathing is a pulse quickening as drops of rain begin to fall.

You want to stay? she asks.

Sure.

You don't mind getting wet? Krysta asks as she reaches her hands up, running her fingers over the curve of his smile.

No.

He leans forward — about to kiss her lips, her cheek, her neck — when a wolf howls, its eerie cry raising the hair on the back of their necks.

You hear that?

The wolf howls again as it begins to rain harder.

They must be hunting, Doug whispers as he pushes himself up to sit on his heels.

Another wolf answers from closer by, in the woods across the field. And another calls from deeper in the woods.

Doug?

Let's get out of here! he says, pulling Krysta to her feet. As they head back in the direction of the fence and the girls' washroom they hear the wolves closing in on the field, one call answering another, weaving a web of uncanny sounds around them.

They find the fence, climb over it, and run up the steps of the girls' washroom. Inside, Doug finds the switch for the street lamp that shines out over the playing field and flicks it on. He looks to Krysta and then sticks his head out the door. The howling has died down with the sudden flooding of light into the tomb-dark night. He looks back at Krysta: I think it's all right now. I'll walk you back to your cabin.

Okay, she says, eyes still wide, her hair wet and tangled, her shirt damp and clinging to her skin.

They won't come near the light. Besides, I don't think they were after us.

No?

Doug kisses Krysta goodnight on the steps of her cabin. And then he heads down the path through the woods towards the maintenance shed. It's pouring now and he's soaked through to the skin by the time he reaches where he thinks the shed should be. But he can hear rain on the water and he realizes he must have taken a wrong turn on the paths in the dark.

He walks for a bit, forgetting about the wolves – assuming that they've given up their hunt to find shelter – and thinking about Krysta. Her body hot against him. The rain coming down on her face. He feels himself going hard again, thinking about where he wished his hands had gone, as he stumbles in the dark over tree roots knotting the path, until he cracks his head against the side of a cabin.

He rubs the top of his head. There's a shuffling sound inside but soon all falls quiet again. He can still hear rain on water, off to his right.

This must be a junior boys' cabin, he thinks as he walks out a bit from the building and leans his back against a tree. Rain is running down his face, off his chin, soaking his shirt and running into his pants, filling his shoes. He fumbles with the zipper of his jeans, yanks it down, and reaches his thumb in to pull his gitch down over his cock, for once in his life not thinking of his father and feeling no shame.

He spits in his right hand and begins rubbing himself, pressing his shoulder bones against the trunk of the tree, rolling his head back and opening his mouth as the tension in his body builds, rainwater mingling with his sweat and running in at the corners of his mouth.

He's right on the edge, ready to let go, when there's a bright flash.

Doug drops his hand, stumbles forwards, blinking, trying to get the sunspots out of his eyes. His cock goes flaccid and he stuffs it back in pants as he tries to find the path and his way back to the maintenance shed, waiting for the thunder to follow the flash of lightning.

But he doesn't hear anything: only the rain pouring down.

Doug wakes up to someone pounding on the door of the maintenance shed. He rubs his eyes, rolls over, and looks at his watch: 7 am. I missed breakfast! he thinks as he rolls out of bed, pulls on a pair of jogging pants and a hoodie and goes to answer the door.

When he opens the door he sees the camp director standing on the porch. He looks to the unfinished picnic table and then to the open can of stain, now filled and diluted with rainwater, sitting by the director's foot.

Douglas!

Yes? he says, snapping his eyes up to hers.

A camper came to me this morning with a digital camera...

This loses Doug. What the hell is she talking about a camera?

It was a junior boy camper who came to me and showed me this picture, she says as she hands him a camera. His first thought is: What kind of rich mom sends a friggin digital camera to camp with her kid? But when he sees the picture his mouth drops and he feels as if his dad has walked into the bathroom and caught him, alone, with his hand in the Vaseline jar.

The picture on the camera is of him, leaning against the tree in the rain, his mouth gaping as if he's in pain, his right hand gripping his cock.

How?

The flash.

Someone took a picture. But who?

Who took this? he asks in barely a whisper.

The boy who you apparently came close to killing the other day in the forest. He says you tried to push a dead tree over on him?

I didn't know he was there.

Whether you knew he was there or not is irrelevant. Behaviour like this, she says as she snatches the camera from his hand, cannot be tolerated. Not when it's done within sight of young campers. What would a parent say if they saw this on their child's camera?

I...I...I didn't...

This cannot be explained or excused away, she says, wagging the camera at him.

But–

Pack your bags. A taxi has already been called, she says as she turns on her heel and steps off the porch. Don't bother cleaning this up. Just pack and bring your stuff down to the camp office in twenty minutes.

With that she turns and stomps down the path.

Doug stands there frozen, unable to think about anything except the barbed-wire fact that he is going home to his dad.

He packs slowly, fisting his clothes into his tote. Gitch, socks, jeans, T-shirts ...

He looks up at the caricature of his dad. He turns and spits on the floor, places the lid on his tote and snaps its edges down. He stands up so he is face to face with his dad's cartoon. As he stares at the image of his father his hands start to tremble and his arms begin to shake.

The shaking spreads through his whole body until he is almost convulsing: waves of anger crashing over him until he turns and runs to the counter, grabs his homemade hammer and hurls it across the room as his father's cartooned face. The hammer hits handle-first and breaks – the rusty head hitting the floor like a large tossed stone.

Doug looks at the broken hammer and then up at the drawing on the wall; his dad stares back at him, almost grinning. Doug grabs his tote in two hands, walks to the door, and leaves after dropping his set of keys on the workbench.

Doug waits outside the office, sitting on his tote. Bill Smithwick, the canoe trip leader, stops and asks why he's going home. He doesn't answer, only motions with his head toward the office door. Other counsellors come by and ask similar questions; most of the time he can't even lift his head to look at them, let alone answer. He keeps hoping Krysta will come around the corner. He wants to see her before the taxi comes to take him back.

But she doesn't come around the corner or up from the waterfront. Everyone else seems to pass by him, sitting outside the office on his tote. Even the boy he almost killed walks past him, coming out of the cookery. The kid walks right past him, stops at the corner of the building, turns and holds up his digital camera and snaps another picture of Doug. The kid looks at the image on his camera, smiles malevolently and looks up at Doug. Then he disappears around the corner.

Doug hangs his head. He closes his eyes and doesn't open them until he hears a car drive up in front of the office. He looks up to see a taxi turning around. The director comes out and sees him into the cab, gives the driver the camp Visa number and a photocopy of directions to Doug's house.

The camp director looks into the back of the cab at Doug but doesn't say anything. She says thank you to the cab driver who puts the car in gear and pulls away. The cab winds its way up the driveway that snakes away from the camp, through the woods and out to the road.

But as the cabby is passing the boys'. washroom, Krysta runs out from along the path from the maintenance shed. She has something in her hand: a bundle. She's waving it at the taxi driver who jerks to a halt. Doug rolls down his window and Krysta passes him the bundle wrapped in old paint rags and duct tape.

I found it, she pants, reaching for his hand through the window.

We got to go, buddy, the driver says.

Your number? Doug asks.

I'll get yours from the office and call.

Okay.

The cab begins to pull away.

Bye! Krysta says as she squeezes Doug's hand quickly and lets go, pulling her hand out the window as the cabby speeds up a little.

Doug turns and waves out the rear window, but the cabby turns the corner into the woods and Krysta is gone. He turns in his seat and looks at the crudely wrapped bundle on his lap. He peels off the duct tape and pulls back the folds of the old paint rags.

The hammer he had hurled into the forest days ago sits on his lap. He grips its handle in his right hand and turns it over, back and forth, flexing his fingers around its shaft as the cabby pulls out onto the main road and accelerates.

EIGHT-BALL

As Harold orders another whisky he has a premonition, but he doesn't recognize himself as the deer in the flash of vision, with its side blasted open, staggering, lurching and snorting blood onto white November snow.

"When will you be back?" Harold's father asked from under the Chevette.

Harold dug his left hand farther into his jeans pocket, fiddling the nine twenty-dollar bills – his violin case in his right hand. "I'll come back to visit ... after."

"After what?" his dad asked, voice strained as he tried to wrench the rusted oil plug loose. "Friggin Carl could've drained the oil before he let this piece of crap car rust in his yard," he grunted.

"After I make it big."

"After you – Frig!" his dad spit as the plug came loose

and he got a splash of oil in his eye. "Friggin piece of scrap metal!" he cursed as he rolled out from under the car, kicked the drain pan under the little stream of black oil, and rubbed his eyes with the corner of his shirt.

"You okay?"

"What do you care, Marilyn?"

"I said I'll be back after, eh?"

"Go on then." His dad turned and kicked the fender of the car with his steel-toed boot. He didn't turn back to his son but said, "You're going to miss the hunt. All for your friggin music. What do I tell Dan and the others, eh? My Goth son got tired of his little black hole of a room and set out for the friggin city?"

Harold stood there silently, thinking about his basement room and how he'd painted it black to see if he could get a rise out of his dad — a teenage challenge to the beatings he got as a kid. But his dad hadn't said anything to him. And he thought of how neither of his parents had really talked to him since. Except for quips about him being a Goth — even though he never wore leather, painted his nails black, or listened to heavy metal. He thought about how, during the past few months, he'd lie on his bed from Friday night to Monday morning and no one would call him or tell him to come for supper or ask him to help in the garage. It seemed funny to him that his dad actually wanted him to stay for the hunt. But, then again, the hunt was the only time of year his dad ever really seemed alive; throughout the rest of the year he'd sit in an old broken lazy-boy out in his shop while Harold lay like a corpse on his bed in the basement, surrounded by pitch black walls.

Harold had looked for months at his violin sitting in the corner of his dark room. He hadn't played it since his grandpa — who'd given it to him and taught him how to play — had died of lung cancer, a year back, after a long fight with the disease.

"So what am I to tell the guys, eh? When I go into the camp this year?"

"Tell them I'm going to make it big."

"You think you're that good, do ya? Eh, Manson?"

"Grandpa said I was."

"Your grandpa only ever played that friggin violin when he was drunk off his ass."

Harold didn't answer. He knew he played best when he was drunk too but his mom had been going to the Pentecostal Church since camp meeting time in July and had been doing her best to keep the house dry. Said it was for his dad's health. There hadn't been a beer in the fridge since August and it'd been that long since he'd played his violin. But he wasn't going to let his dad talk him out of leaving for the city. It'd taken him three months to get up the gumption to peel himself off his bed. It's either get out or give up, he had thought as he packed a backpack of clothes, put the violin in its case, and stuffed the nine twenty-dollar bills in his pocket. If he could just get to Toronto he'd be able to land a bar gig — that was the only thing in his life, at that moment, that he was certain of. His dad would say he was naive if he told him; he always told Harold he was like a big grown-up kid — that's why he wouldn't tell his dad his plan, because if he voiced it, it might evaporate, like morning mist on Mud Lake out behind their house.

"I'm going to make it, Dad," he said before he turned and walked out of the garage. He headed down the driveway to the road and stuck out his thumb at a passing car.

His dad limped out of the shop and yelled down the drive to him: "I bet your mom twenty bucks you'd be back before Christmas! Told her you'd wuss out in less than a month and come crawling back to work in the shop!"

"Can't fix the world with a wrench, Dad," Harold muttered as he saw a white Mustang crest the hill, headed along West Coon Lake Road towards Highway 62.

The driver slowed down as he approached Harold. Just before Harold stepped into the car he turned and looked once more at his dad. He wanted to give him the finger but he turned, got in the Mustang, slammed the door on his father's yelling, and felt himself pushed back against the leather seat as the young driver floored it.

"Where you going?" the driver asked, shifting gears.

"Close to Toronto as you can get me."

Harold shakes his head to clear it of the premonition and then looks out the window of O'Grady's Tap and Grill, across the street and down the bricked lane of King's College Road, to the distant, ornately chiseled edifice of University College. December rain is mizzling outside and he sees people walking back and forth under umbrellas or hunkered in long dark raincoats.

The world's moving quick, he thinks as he sits stone still.

You going to drink and get out? the waiter asks him.

Harold looks down at his half-empty pint and then to the thirteen empty shot glasses he's set up circled around the salt shaker. He doesn't remember coming into the bar nor what he was doing beforehand. He looks over at the bartender who seems to be swaying in his vision.

He opens his mouth to speak but lets out a loud belch instead.

Finish it and get out. You've had your limit, bud.

I'm not yer blud, Harold slurs as he holds up his glass, looks out the window at the university and says, Here's to makin it big. After which he pounds the half pint back, stands shakily to his feet and heads for the door, muttering, Liquor before bleer yer in the clear!

You forgot your wrench, man! the waiter calls to Harold, who is halfway out the door. The young clean-shaven guy walks over to Harold and hands him the shiny new monkey wrench and asks: So what're you going to fix with this?

I'm good at fixin things, Harold mumbles as he staggers out onto the sidewalk. Goin to go fix things. As he says this he looks up and realizes the rain has stopped. Going to go play for him, he whispers to no one in particular.

"Listen, guy," the short, spiky-haired bar-owner said to Harold in the alley behind the pub. *"You need cover tunes, okay? And a back-up band. Violin's great if you're Stravinsky or some crazy stunt like Ashley MacIsaac's. Hey! There's an idea, Virtuoso..."*

"Harold."

"Whatever! Listen, guy, if you pick up tap-dancing and wear a kilt, I'll think about it. Boozers love that East Coast crap."

"I can't dance."

"Then you can't play in my bar. Sorry, guy. Better luck down the road maybe."

Harold blinked as the bar-owner slammed the back door of the pub. He looked down at his violin case. "Thought people liked fiddle music," he breathed as he headed down the alley towards the next bar on the street.

Dude! Watch out!

Horns blare. Brakes screech. Tires skid.

Harold hears yelling. People shout at him. He looks up and sees the silver chrome letters MACK on the grill of a big dump truck a foot from his face. He glances drunkenly about him. Cars are stopped. Horns are blaring. People are leaning out their windows, shouting and waving fists.

Get off the street, man!

He blinks, looks up, and tries to hold the distant edifice of University College steady in his blurred vision as he stumbles forward off the road and hears car tires squeal behind him as people take off. He hears the dump truck grind into gear and roar to life as it drives away.

Blood pounds in his ears. His eyes are watering. He rubs them with the grimy sleeve of his canvas work coat. And then he heads down King's College Road, his feet scuffing over the brick cobblestones.

"You can't just set up and play here," a man in blue jeans and a black coat, with a French beret pulled down over his grey hair, said to Harold in the subway tunnel

under College Street, on the west side of University.

"Why?" Harold dropped his violin from his shoulder and held it in his left hand. He looked at the older man who stood before him, leaning on a battered guitar case plastered with Dean Markley stickers.

"It's my turf, boy."

"Name's Harold."

"I don't care what your name is. You can't just set up and play in a hot-spot like this. For one, you need a ticket from the city. And I've been busking for twenty years around here; I've earned this spot."

"Could play with you," Harold offered hopefully as he rubbed his frayed bow against his dirty orange toque.

"Know any popular songs?"

"Squid Jiggin Reel?"

"Eh?"

"I know reels and jigs. A few hymns."

"I do rock n' roll and blues. Sorry, boy." The older man set down his guitar case and opened it. Harold looked at the man dumbly as he felt a gust of wind come up from the underground.

"Morning rush coming now," said the man as he pulled out his Vendor six-string, slung it over his shoulder, and started tuning. He didn't look up at Harold, who stood staring at him, but he said, "Try the streets."

The man started strumming as Harold packed away his violin. A crowd was coming towards the stairs. Harold straightened up and fell in step with the throng as people began to pass him by. The old busker behind him sang "Gonna Hypnotize a Million" as Harold mounted the steps *on the south side of College. When he got to street-level and stepped out onto the sidewalk, he felt cold early-November rain spit in his face.*

An East Indian girl whispers to her boyfriend as they sidestep Harold in front of the Graduate English Department: I think he's drunk.

Harold glances sideways at the girl who grips her boyfriend's hand tighter at the sight of the drunken man's blood-shot eyes. He hears the girl's boyfriend say something in a language he doesn't understand.

Fuggin rich-ass immigrants, he mumbles as he trudges past the Gerstein Library. He smells coffee and salami and he remembers how Ziggy would make coffee in at the hunting camp: how he'd make it so strong it'd make Harold's eyes water and his heart race. He stops for a second and looks at a small Oriental girl standing beside a bench, eating a sandwich with one hand and holding a Starbucks coffee cup in the other.

The girl stops chewing at the sight of the scruffy-faced man in the dirty work coat who is staring at her. Everything seems to hold mercifully still in Harold's vision for a brief second. He sniffs for another smell of the salami sandwich, remembering the venison summer sausage his mom made, but all he can smell is cigarette smoke, exhaust, and his own stink that clings to him like grease to his jacket.

"Down further, eh!" *said the young Native girl who sat under the bridge by the Union Bus Station, wrapped in a horse-patterned blanket that was scarred with cigarette burns.*

Harold shrugged and plodded farther down the sidewalk under the bridge. He had gut-rot from six shots of Jack Daniel's he bought with the thirty dollars he made busking by the Air Canada Centre. He burped and could taste his own stomach acid mixed with the oaky aftertaste.

Harold trudged towards the far end — away from the girl clicking a dry lighter, trying to get it to spark in order to light up a half-smoked cigarette. He slumped to the floor, holding his violin case in his lap, and immediately fell into a deep sleep.

He slept there for hours: until the last bus left the station and the steady stream of cars driving past him became sporadic. He didn't wake up when a guy in a black leather jacket came and sat beside him. The guy was young but his face was wrinkled like sun-baked lizard skin. He looked over at Harold: watched his chest rise and fall with sleep's even rhythm.

The man looked back and forth to make sure nobody was around. Then he pulled a long needle out from under his jacket. He set it on the ground by his hip and then reached over to push on Harold's arm.

No movement.

The guy smiled as he pulled a piece of soft rubber tubing out of his inner jacket pocket. "How about a speedball, eh?"

The Native girl, wrapped in her horse-patterned blanket and seated several yards away, called out in a cracked whisper to the man in the leather jacket as she held out her scratched and bruised forearm, her fist clenched around a damp cigarette.

The man lifted his chin in response and motioned her over with a shift of his head. Then he elbowed Harold until Harold woke to see the stranger and the Native girl next to him. He was still groggy as he watched the stranger slip a needle into the girl's arm. Her eyes lit up and her head lolled as her teeth let loose the rubber tubing she had synched about her arm. He saw her smile then. No teeth. And she didn't look a day older than eighteen.

The stranger turned to Harold and held up the needle. "One speedball. On the house, my friend. This is a one-time offer."

Harold nodded and rolled up the thick sleeve of his coat. The guy carefully tied the piece of rubber around Harold's forearm, said to pull tight on it. Harold snorted the cold air in a gulp, closed his hand into a fist and then unclenched it. Closed his eyes.

The man waited until Harold was still and breathing evenly. Then he picked the needle up out of the puddle it was sitting in, found a large vein bulging on Harold's arm, took a deep breath, and plunged it in.

Harold's eyes shot open and he jerked his arm into his chest. Looked hazily about. He saw the man in a black leather jacket walking away from him — the Native girl staggering after the guy before she collapsed and curled up on the sidewalk, singing brokenly to no one. He was about to call out but as he opened his mouth the cold solidity of the pavement went out from under him and he felt on the verge of orgasm as he vomited all over himself.

Harold stands on the front steps of University College. People are pushing past him as they come out of the building, which seems to be emptying. Everyone is talking of Christmas break and being finished exams. Harold stands like a rock in the middle of this current of human bodies.

Why am I here? I was here before. But for what?

People spilling out the doors bump into each other as they sidestep to avoid the grungy young man with the patchy beard and sad watering eyes. They can smell the whiffs of alcohol on him and he reeks of rotten orange peels and old grease.

Can I help you? a young girl stops and asks, hugging her books across her chest like a shield between her new suede jacket and Harold's grimy coat.

Can't fix what isn't broke, eh? Harold mumbles.

I could call a cab, the girl offers.

A cab? What good's a cab?

The girl looks around her, embarrassed; then she turns and walks down the steps, as if she just realized how useless her offer really was.

"Name's Neb. Yours?"
"Harold."
"You smell like shit, my friend. You sick last night?"
"Yeah."
"Got something that might make you feel better."
"What?"
"Nickle rocks," Neb said. His wrinkled face cracked in a grotesque grin as he pulled a small plastic bag out of his

jacket pocket. Harold recognized him now as the stranger under the bridge the other night. The one who gave him his first hit.

"What's that?" Harold asked, though he already knew.

"Medicine, my friend. Good fuckin medicine." Neb ran his tongue over his yellowed teeth. "Tasty."

"I don't know."

"It's your fuckin life, man. But this stuff," he said, waving the little plastic bag, "this will make your craptacular life go fuckin technicolour."

"Eh?"

"Don't need nothin when you're on this shit." Neb held up the bag in his left hand and looked at it methodically, like he was going to say something profound. "To be or not to fuckin be," he said, smiling, "Ha! You read any of that stuff in high school?"

"What?"

"Nothing, man. You don't need nothing when you got this. Don't need no house, no bed. Don't even need any fuckin food most of the time."

Harold's nose was plugged so he couldn't smell the acid stench of his own vomit. His hands were a little shaky. And he was cold. "This stuff heat you up?"

"Like jackin off with Rub-A-535."

"What?"

"Better than coffee, my friend. Better than coffee."

"How much?"

"A nickel for five bucks."

"A nickel?"

Neb pulled one of the small white rocks out of the bag. "This," he said, holding up the rock that looked like a little chunk of quartz, "is a nickel-rock."
"Five bucks for that?"
"Best fiver you'll ever spend."
"I don't have any money."
"You have a fuckin fiddle."
"Where do I find you?"
"I'll find you, my friend. I'll find you."

Harold walks in through University College's main portcullis, pushing against the stream of students exiting the building. He stands between two staircases, looking out at the main lobby area, turns and takes the steps to the left.

Lifting each foot for each step is like trudging through the knee-deep slush over the swamps by Spruce Lake, back home in St. Lola – chasing the hounds during the hunt with PJ, Duncan, and his dad. Each step is an effort as he continues to push himself upward.

Neb found him on his way back from the Air Canada Centre. Harold's fingers were blue with cold and his lips were chapped and bleeding.
"You make anything, friend?"
Harold shivered in his coat. "Ya-ya-yeah," he stammered through chattering teeth. "Made s-somethin today."
"Enough for the nickle?"
"T-t-two nickles p-p-please." Harold reached a frostbitten hand into his pocket and fished out two fives.

"Bills?" Neb asked, obviously used to being handed small change from street bums like Harold.

"M-m-made fifteen and b-b-bought a hotdog."

Neb nodded and glanced around and then looked over Harold's shoulder.

"Great. Enough talk, okay? Here's a dime. Keep busking and you'll keep warm all winter, my friend." Neb snatched the two fives from Harold's shaking hand, shoved a small baggy at him and then spun on his heel and jogged away, leaving Harold alone in the street, longing for warmth in his bones and thinking of how every night of the hunt PJ would make a big fire before they'd all crawl into their sleeping bags in the loft — his father always on the far side of the room from him.

Harold stumbles onto the second floor landing. The air feels like water around him and for a moment he thinks he's fallen through the ice on the swamps near Spruce Lake.

He thrashes his arms and then suddenly stops and looks down at his hands — the right empty and the left fisted around the monkey wrench. He turns his right hand over, gazes at the palm and then squints at his wrinkled lifeline. He'd been clenching his fist all the way up the stairs and his palm is sweaty: the skin like that of a rotten crabapple.

An Oriental student walks out of the East Wing, crosses in front of Harold, glancing sideways at him in disgust, and then disappears into the West Wing. Harold drops his hands and looks about suspiciously.

Friggin chinks.

And then for some reason he jerks his glance upward,

feeling as if some malevolent set of eyes is looking down on him. All he sees is a large metal abstract sculpture suspended from the ceiling. But Harold doesn't know it is art; to him it looks like a massive guillotine, like in one of the slasher films his dad used to watch.

Harold felt as if the top might fly right off his head as the frozen fingers of his left hand flew over the violin strings, his right hand slid and jerked the bow, and his foot stomped out the rhythm of his reel as he sucked hard on his fourth dime-rock of the day.

People were starting to crowd around the air-vent he was standing on; they were throwing nickels, dimes, quarters, and loonies into his open fiddle case. The reel ended when the last bit of crack dissolved in his mouth. He dropped the violin to his side and looked around at the gathered crowd with wild blood-shot eyes and a creepy, exhilarated smile.

Nobody clapped. Everyone looked away from Harold's crazy, twitching grin; they all turned and left. Leaving him to pocket his change, pack up his fiddle, and head off to find Neb. He needed more dimes, more hits – more.

For the music.

He found he played better when he was high and that brought in more cash, which purchased more crack, which fuelled his music – more.

That was his reasoning as he walked back in the direction of the bridge by the GO Bus Terminal. Cars whizzing past him were brightly coloured blurs to his eyes. And the sidewalk seemed to rise and fall and made him feel as if he was walking on a sea of liquid concrete.

When he arrived at the bridge his hands were starting to shake. He pushed past the Native girl who was curled up under her horse-patterned blanket, snoring and intermittently talking in her sleep to someone named Jaz.

Harold pushed past her to his spot by the other end of the bridge. When he got there he sat down on the cold concrete, not feeling anything except the fire in his bones. He leaned his head back against the stone wall. As the cocaine began to wear off he could feel the dampness seeping through his pants, shrivelling his nut sack.

The smile slipped from his face and he looked down at his brown shoes stained with road salt; he wiggled his damp toes inside but could barely feel them. He began rubbing his arms, but as he did so he felt something like spiders crawling up his skin, inside his coat. He slapped his arms but could still feel them moving up past his elbows, over his shoulders and down his spine and chest and into his pants. He jumped to his feet, ripped off his jacket and began tearing at the skin of his arms with cracked, uncut fingernails.

He scraped and scratched until blood began to ooze to the surface, but he could still feel the spiders crawling all over him, burrowing under his skin. He tore at himself as he rubbed his back against the wall. And then, as suddenly as it started, it stopped.

Harold looked up and saw Neb leaning against the wall, smiling.

"Coke bugs, eh?" he said, licking his yellow teeth.

"What?"

"Just a hallucination, my friend."

"A what?"

"You'll get used to them. A hardcore user like you shouldn't be afraid of a few imaginary bugs. It's been what? Three weeks or so? Guys like you usually stay on the nickels for months or even years. But most guys doing it don't got talent." Neb nudges his toe against Harold's violin case. *"They say it's good for artists and shit."*

"It is?"

"Got a list of big-shot users at my place."

"Famous people?" Harold asked, his arms folded across his chest. He looked down at the scratches on his arms that were beginning to cauterize in the cold.

"Famous and fuckin historical."

"Like?" Harold asked as he bent to pick up his jacket and put it on.

"Like that Sir Conan guy."

"The barbarian?"

"No! Not friggin Schwarzenegger! I'm talking about the guy who made up that detective Sherlock Holmes. He was a crack-head and his character was a crack-head. In those days crack-heads were the detectives and now the detectives are after the crack-heads. It's messed, my friend. We live in the wrong century."

Harold stared dumbly at Neb. *"Can I get anything stronger for forty?"*

Neb looked at Harold, raised his eyebrows in disbelief, and then cracked an ugly grin. *"For fifty I can get you an eight-ball; that's a one-time only discount rate, mind you."* He licked his rotting teeth.

"What's an eight-ball?"

"Eighth of an ounce, my friend. Powder."

"Oh."

"Give me the money and I'll get you the stuff."

Harold was about to hand over the pocketful of coins, but he balked when he put his hand inside and felt just how full his pocket was: three days' worth of busking. He looked up at Neb, who was looking at Harold's pocketed hand. "You bring me the eight-ball and I'll buy it."

"What?" Neb's eyes snapped up angrily.

Harold looked down at his shoes but didn't take his hand out of his pocket. "Bring it and I'll buy it."

"You gonna have the money when I get back?" Neb asked and then spit on the ground between them.

"Yeah."

"Okay, my friend," Neb said, his lips curled in a sneer. "But don't screw around. I bring the goods you'd better have the cash or I'll break your fuckin knees with a baseball bat. See you tomorrow around eleven. Right here." With that, Neb spit again, turned and walked out from under the bridge into the cold, early December night.

Harold sat on the cold sidewalk, leaned his head against the wall and thought for a brief moment about spending the money on a train ticket home. He shivered in the cold and tried to put the thought out of his mind.

Harold hears piano music coming from the West Wing as he lunges forward onto the landing, out from under the sculpture he takes for a guillotine, and almost knocks a girl over. The girl tries to pull away but Harold has a hold of her arm with his right hand and is using her to steady himself. She starts to scream but is silenced by his blood-shot stare.

Ya know Dr. Richmond? Harold slurs.

The girl just nods her head, terrified of the big bearded guy holding her arm in one hand and a monkey wrench in the other.

Where is he?

The girl points to the stairs behind Harold. He's up there, she says, Preparing for his concert tonight ... over at Hart House.

Can you go get him for me?

Who are you?

I was ... was ... gonna be his ... student.

I'll go get him for you, the girl says, wide-eyed.

Harold lets go of her and she steps around him and goes up the stairs, glancing back at him over her shoulder until she disappears.

Harold looks about him, goes to the railing and glances over. People are milling below. He shrugs and heads towards the music coming from the hall off to his left.

He stops at the door of the West Wing and then enters the hall. The room is huge and long with a high ceiling that almost makes Harold fall over backwards as he cranes his head back to take in the solid oak beams. He holds the door for balance and looks to the far end of the room.

The Oriental guy who passed Harold in the hall is playing the grand piano there; his back is to Harold, who wanders over and sits in a chair on the south side of the room, facing the great round, blue stained-glass window. He looks up at the large stained-glass circle and he feels as if a big sad eye is staring down at him.

He looks down from the God's Eye window and pulls the eight-ball of speed that he had bought from Neb out of his pocket. It's in a small plastic bag. More potent, Neb had told him, than regular cocaine. Parachute it, he'd said, parachute it and you'll land in a fuckin psychedelic Eden. Paradise, man. Nirvana.

Night came and the temperature dropped well below zero. Harold hugged his knees as he sat curled up under the bridge. His whole body shook with cold and withdrawal. He had bought a sleeping bag from the Salvation Army a week ago, but somebody nabbed it from under the bridge when he went off to the Air Canada Centre to busk one day.

Eventually he got up and walked stiffly, violin case in one hand, past the Native girl and around the corner to the GO Bus Terminal: 19:06 read the nearest digital platform sign. Just after seven, Harold thought after he counted on his fingers from twelve to nineteen.

He thought he saw his friend Bill Smithwick getting on a bus bound for Barrie. He looked at the sign above him to recheck the time, but when he looked down again the man was gone. Harold headed for the door that opened onto a set of stairs; the stairs led up to Union Station's Platform 1 and to another flight of stairs that led down into Union Station itself.

Once inside Union, Harold headed past the GO ticket booths and the Second Cup store towards the subway. He crossed over to the TTC building, bought a subway token with some of his change and went down the escalator to the subway platform.

He stood at the base of the escalator asking for spare change for a bit, and then he boarded the northbound train to Downsview and got off at Queen's Park.

As the train pulled away he headed for the escalator at the other end of the platform. He climbed the stairs and turned down the tunnel towards the west side of University. The old grey-haired busker who'd ousted him that one day wasn't there. So he pulled out his violin, carefully tuned the strings, and started to play an old hymn his grandfather had taught him when he first gave Harold the violin. His grandpa played jigs and reels when he was sober but he played best when he was drunk, when he'd play old hymns out of the Free Methodist Psalter.

Harold's hands were shaky and the music was rough, like an unsanded pine-plank floor – like the floor in the hunting camp. He felt the warm breeze of the underground blow up the tunnel and around him as he imagined the warmth and glow of the fire in the cabin's hearth during hunting season, singing over and over in his head, as if trying to convince himself, "It is well, it is well ..."

He had totally forgotten where he was when he heard a guy's effeminate voice in front of him. "You like violin music, eh?"

Harold stopped playing and stared at the guy in front of him who was wearing tight jeans, a suit jacket, green scarf and a fedora that was too small for his head. "Eh?"

"If you like violin music you should come and hear my music prof play. Here," he said as he handed Harold a xeroxed poster. "It's tomorrow evening if you're interested."

"Thanks," Harold said as he looked at the poster.

The guy in the fedora said, "No problem," and turned and headed down the tunnel towards the subway. Harold held up the poster he'd been given:

MOZART AND EAST COAST CLASSICS
AN ECLECTIC EVENING OF MUSIC
WITH INTERNATIONALLY RENOWNED VIOLINIST
AND PROFESSOR OF MUSIC AT U OF T'S
UNIVERSITY COLLEGE
DR. DONALD RICHMOND
7 PM AT THE HART HOUSE THEATRE

Harold's thoughts raced. He could get by busking but maybe if this guy heard him play he could finally make it. *I just need to meet him*, Harold thought, *just need to meet him and play for him and I'll be able to fix things. Have something to show Dad when I go home for Christmas.*

He was so happy with his plan that he packed up his violin, raced up the steps to street-level on the north side of College, and whistled as he walked down the sidewalk towards King's College Road, looking for a windless alley to spend the night in.

Harold unfolds a small square of rolling paper. Then he pulls out the little plastic baggy containing the eighth of an ounce of amphetamine. He tries to pour the powder onto the small square of paper but his hands are shaking and he spills some on the desk. He brushes as much as he can onto the paper then licks his index finger and rubs it over the excess traces on the desk. Then he starts rubbing his gums with it.

Gummy a bit of it, Neb had said, and fuckin parachute the rest.

He licks his finger clean and then sits back, feeling the rush of blood warm his ears like a first gulp of strong coffee, the way Bill's uncle Ziggy used to make it in at the hunting camp by boiling a handful of grounds in a small pot of water and straining the tar-black drink into tin cups.

Harold found another nickel-rock in his coat pocket as he was waiting to talk to the secretary who was supposed to know where this Dr. Richmond was. Just as he popped it in his mouth the secretary asked if she could help him. He crunched down on the chunk of crack, swallowed and asked: "Can I talk to Dr. Richmond?"

"And you are?"

"Ah, well ... I wanted to play for him."

"Play?" the secretary asked as she took off her glasses, sat back in her swivel chair behind her desk. "Play what?"

"Uh ... the violin."

"You want to play for Dr. Richmond?" she asked with a bit of a smirk. "Your name?"

"Harold. Harold Lazarus Witaker."

Harold looked around him as the secretary said, "Well, Mr. Witaker ..."

The clock read 10:30 am. He saw a girl in a jean mini-skirt walk into the office and slouch down in the chairs behind him, so he tried to whisper as he said, "Yeah. I'd like to play for him." *Harold glanced over his shoulder at the girl and then added,* "In his office." *He could feel the* high hitting his head and he had to grab the secretary's desk to keep his hands from trembling.

"Well, sir," the secretary said, pretending to look at the calendar on the wall, "I don't think Dr. Richmond will be able to hear you play today."

"Tomorrow?"

"No, not likely. You see Dr. Richmond is an extremely busy man and sometimes he doesn't have time to see his own graduate students, let alone... someone like yourself."

The rush was hitting Harold now: his pupils dilated and his hands shook as he let go of the secretary's desk and thrust them deep into his coat pockets. "I'll play for you!" he blurted out as he glanced nervously around the office.

"That won't be necessary."

"I'll play for you and you tell Dr. Richmond about me," he said quickly as he bent over, opened his fiddle case with quivering hands and pulled out his violin and bow.

The secretary was sitting forward in her chair now, straightening her glasses on her nose, "Sir, we can't have random people auditioning—"

"One song!" Harold snapped.

The girl behind him giggled as he was putting his violin to his ear to tune.

Harold jerked around and almost dropped his violin. He glared at the girl, who had her feet up on the coffee table; her knees were bent and slightly apart. Harold was about to yell at her: ask her what her problem was. But he just stared up her skirt as the little triangle of purple underwear.

The corners of the girl's smile dropped as she put her

feet down and stood up, snapping Harold out of his trance.

The girl stomped out of the office.

Harold wanted to yell but instead he tucked the instrument under his chin and began angrily to play his out-of-tune violin, savagely sawing the bow and batting it off the strings.

"Get out!" the secretary yelled over the ruckus but Harold didn't hear her. So she picked up her phone and dialed campus security.

Harold continued to play and as the high reached its apex his left hand moved faster over the strings and his right hand pumped the bow harder, filling the office and the hallway of the college with the horrible sound of a grown man screaming in agony.

He played until two security guards came and dragged him yelling and cursing from the college and threw him onto the pavement of King's College Circle, where they told him to leave the campus before they called the police.

"I was trying to fix things!" Harold yelled as he picked himself up from the pavement. "I was trying to fix things!" And then he turned and ran away with his violin in hand, down the lane, under the bridge and to Queen's Park, trying to find the subway so he could get back to Neb.

Harold is half listening to the Oriental guy playing a classical piece on the piano. He looks up at the back of the student, watching the guy's straight black hair bounce a little on his head as he pulses the keys on the low end of the piano, drumming a rhythm of low chords, fingering towards the high end: the sound filling the all-but-empty room.

As the music builds, Harold drops his head and looks down at the little mound of powdered amphetamine on the small square of rolling paper on the desk in front of him. He's not sure if it's the music getting to him or the speed he's gummied finally hitting his head, but his eyes start to sting and he shuts them tight, squeezing out sticky tears.

When he opens his eyes he looks down again, sniffs and rolls the paper, holds it up to his lips and licks it, pastes it together with his spit, and then folds the ends in over each other. He holds the little wad of paper between his forefinger and thumb, looks at it, smiles weakly, and then pops it into his mouth where he rolls it around and around, lubricating it with his saliva, before tossing his head back and sinking the eight-ball down his esophagus.

"You got it?" Harold asked Neb as he approached him under the bridge.

"You been crying, princess?" Neb asks as he looks at the tear stains on Harold's scruffy, dirty face.

"No," Harold says as he rubs the back of his hand over his eyes. "It's just cold is all."

"Oh. Well, you're late."

"Had to catch the subway."

"Did, did you?"

"Yeah, went to ... to ..."

"To what?"

"To meet ... someone," Harold said, trying to stare Neb in the eyes. "About my music."

"Big fuckin whoop, my friend. You got fifty?"

Harold pulled the change out of his pocket and bent

over to count it out on the ground but Neb grabbed the corner of his coat and dragged him back to his feet.

"What the fuck you doing? Want some ass-wipe driving by to 911 the cops on his cell cause he thinks he sees some homeless bum counting out change for a dealer?"

Harold just raised his eyebrows. "You don't want to count it?"

"Give it here," Neb said as he handed Harold a ziplock bag. "Dump it. I'll count it, find you later and tell you what you owe, okay?"

"How will you find me?"

"I'm like Mephistopheles, my friend. Like the fuckin wind. I'll find you."

"Sure," Harold said, not understanding the allusion. He dumped a fistful of coins into the ziplock. He emptied his pockets and handed the plastic bag back to Neb.

"Nice doing business."

"Thanks," Harold breathed as Neb handed him a small plastic bag tied with a twist-tie. "This an eight-ball?"

"You can call it that, my friend. Better than cocaine, that stuff. It's amphetamine—"

"Amphetamine?"

"Speed. More kick per buck right there. Just got my holiday shipment. Happy Hanukkah, eh?" Neb said and laughed as he turned, ducked his head against the cold wind blowing under the bridge, and walked away.

When Dr. Richmond enters the West Wing he hears Rachmaninoff's Piano Concerto Number Two in C minor,

Opus 18, being played by one of his Korean students on the piano at the far end of the room, but what he sees first is a tall young bearded man in a grimy work coat standing on a chair off to his left, pretending to play a monkey wrench as if it were a violin.

You there! Dr. Richmond says to Harold.

Harold doesn't hear but continues to rock and sway, immersed in the boiling waters of an acidic high more toxic than any he's yet experienced.

Dr. Richmond looks out the door to where the girl who had fetched him had been standing, but she's gone. Probably too scared to have told anyone as she ran from the building, he thinks as he turns back to the filthy young man miming that he's playing a fiddle.

Hello? Dr. Richmond says as he steps over and tugs on the corner of Harold's jacket to get his attention. The Korean student plays on, oblivious to the scene behind him, which is drowned out by his pounding attempt to master Rachmaninoff.

Harold, feeling something pulling at his jacket, looks down and sees a frizzy-haired older man in a black trench coat standing below him, looking up at him with confused eyes through thick glasses, mystified. Harold is breathing hard as he jumps off the chair – the music and drugs raging in him. He stands shakily on the ground, a head above the professor.

Are you Dr. Richmond? Harold asks.

Yes, says the professor, looking into Harold's smouldering eyes, perceiving a fury in them but not understanding the source or direction of the young man's anger. I'm Dr. Richmond, the professor says. And you are?

Harold.

Okay, Harold, why did you want to see me?

In answer Harold hefts the monkey wrench in his right hand and heaves it down on the professor's sweat-glossed forehead.

Harold found out earlier that night that a ticket to Belleville would cost him $32.86. He thought of the money he handed over to Neb for the eight-ball. At that point, standing between McDonald's and Second Cup in Union Station, he had no desire to go out into the cold and busk for the money. At that moment, he wanted nothing more than to go home. But he needed money. And he needed something, a gift maybe, to appease his dad.

The violin felt heavy in his hand. He shifted his weight from one foot to the other, wondering how much he could get for it at a pawn shop. His desire to go home was quickly whitewashing the value of this family heirloom.

He headed out into the cold, looking for a pawnshop. He found one on Dundas Street West. The pawnbroker looked the violin over for a while, pointed out a number of dints in the wood, and eventually gave Harold eighty-five dollars.

Harold stumbled out into the street, counting his money and then pocketing it as he searched for a hardware store or someplace he could buy a new tool for his dad. Someone told him about a place on Yonge, north of Bloor, so he walked north along Bathurst to Bloor and then east, through the dark shadows cast by the high-rise buildings on Bloor and against the wind that whistled down that street like a damned soul, to Yonge Street, where he eventually found the hardware store.

He bought a monkey wrench for $35.83.

He walked out of the store, cut across to Queen's Parkway and started heading south towards Union Station.

I might even be able to catch a train this evening, he thought as he followed University south on the west side of Queen's Park — the trees there leaning towards him in the wind, their branches extended and reaching like so many hands trying to stop him, but he turned his face from the wind and the trees and pushed on south, past Wellesley towards College.

But when he was standing on the corner of College and University, the collar of his coat turned up because it had started to rain, he was handed a small flyer that read:

THREE BUCKS PER SHOT, FRIDAY SPECIAL AT O'GRADY'S. HAPPY HOLIDAYS!

"Where's this?" Harold asked the man.

"Down there." The man motioned down College towards Spadina.

Maybe I'll have one, Harold thought, *to celebrate going home.*

The sudden crack of bone sounds in Harold's ears like the first clap in a round of applause that erupts in his head. He looks around the big empty room but to him it's filled with people calling his name, cheering him, and clapping. He hears music. His prelude. He holds tight to what he takes to be his violin and walks out the door, feeling as if he's dragging a great weight behind him. The applause follows him out of the West Wing and drums in his ears like a racing heartbeat as he casts a glance over the railing of the second floor landing. The bouquet of roses bleeding red all over his hands – thorns pricking his skin like spider bites – is heavy as a body as he heaves it to the crowd he imagines below, applauding still, continually applauding as he descends the stairs and walks out the door into what he takes to be his open-air amphitheater.

The place is darkening, lit dimly by yellow lights on posts circling his grassy stage, as he steps across the drive, clutching his instrument tightly, feeling his heart pounding so hard he thinks his ribs will shatter. He steps onto the lawn of King's College Circle, hearing the many voices yelling at him as the lights come up blue and red and flashing.

Hands clap like car doors slamming shut as he raises his instrument to his chin and begins to play "It is well, It Is WELL with MY SOUL!"

He plays like a mad man, his fingers sliding over the neck of his instrument like they're slippery with blood, his other hand pumping an invisible bow to draw out music he's never known was in him, thinking as the song crescendos in his mind, feeling as if it will swell his brain and explode his skull: Dad! Look at me! I'm front page news!

There's a flash of light. Pain in his head, his knees. His arms being twisted behind him. His face in the mud, his mouth full of dirt and the blood that's running out of his nose. He tries to look up but a hand is on the back of his head, grinding his face into the earth.

BECOMING MARIA

I usually dream of a silver-haired woman, but in this dream Jesus is kissing me a deep throaty kiss of longing and I'm kissing back, but barely. Wondering how the silver-haired woman slipped into the skin of this ugly man with his scarred face and patchy beard who looks as if he's walked through hell, and who I know — I don't know how I know — is Jesus.

— Maria!

Shoot up out of the dream and crack my forehead off the timbers of the camp bunk overhead.

— Maria, the bell's gone and the girls are in the showers!
— Yeah?
— You coming, girl?

Almost, if not for the fishhook wakeup call. Girl? Girls. Toothbrushing bodywashing is-my-hair-all-right bitter bandying about boys and not wanting to eat breakfast.

– Maria girl, you up or dead?

Always extremes with Shannelle: either have to be alive or dead in her world. No purgatory, like this morning. All mornings. A toe-curling yawn. Stretch white skin over white bones.

– Maria!

I'll have a double espresso of that Scarborough black energy she siphons from some crazy spirit world where angels are morning people. I got a racist in the attic no one knows about. But everyone does, eh? Worst bigot is the person who hates bigots. You're going wingnuts, woman. Keep laying down lies and you dyke-out the truth and make yourself a field of tulips. Lips? Lips kissing my ankles as toes dig in the dirt. A patch of earth to stand on. Orgasm of being alive.

– Girl! You coming, Sleeping Beauty?

And beauty I am not. But wet? O my gawd, what a wacky dream, dude! Dude? The word's funny in my mouth. Like fuck. Like a sausage. Gag me. Come on, I mean really. Who eats those tubes of cartilage musclefat? Gross me out the door.

Out-the-door
Out-the-door
I-need-to-get-my-ass
Out-the-door
Before ...

What rhymes with before? Floor. Under my feet and cold! Where are my shoes? Slippershoes, slip shoes on. Sloppylooking. Sleepy, slickskinned and sweaty. Like *his* face. The scarfaced hippy Jesus in my dream. Crazy dream. Wasn't sure if it was one at first, cause I haven't dreamed of men since I started dating Kevin. But it had to have been a dream. Cause I was beautiful.

The girls think I'm queer, which isn't too far off maybe. But it's the way they look at me when I'm up on the lifeguard tower, which could be because of the way I look at them. I try not to be too conspicuous, but they're beautiful, even at fourteen. Not skinny albino-skinned and blonde as a baby, like me.
 — Okay! Out of the water, girls!
Krysta can be a bit bitchy-sounding, now that she's head lifeguard. But she's nice most of the time. Grumpy since last summer after Doug was sent home. Think they had something going but he got caught wacking off in the forest or something. What would they do if they caught me some nights? I keep what I do quiet though. Hide the razor blades and wear long-sleeved shirts. Modest young Mennonite that I am.
 — Maria?
 — Yeah.
 — You got waterside clean-up?
 — Sure thing.
She's put on weight this year, but she holds it well: all in the hips. I got canoe paddles for hips. All woodeny bone with a white sunburnt skin varnish. Stupid-wet-lifejackets left lying everywhere. Seriously. One stray red flip-flop. Wait a sec. Those are feet on the barge.
 — Hello?
No answer. Think we got a sunsleeper here. Step, step

lightly now. And underneath Muskoka chair number one:
— Bill?
— Yeah? says a groggy red-faced Bill as he rolls over and looks up at me, hand over his eyes to shield them from the sun.
— You burning here?
— Eh?
Why does everyone up Bancroft way say eh? A north-of-seven rural thing, maybe. Baaaa! Why do Scots wear kilts? Cause sheep are afraid of zippers.
— What was that? Bill asks.
— You burning here? I smile. One thing I got is a pearly Julia Roberts smile. Kind of cracks my face in half though. Like hey! Like my teeth? Teeeth! Yeah, that's right. Look at the smile, love the smile, work it, baby ... and ... ok-ay, have passed into silentawkward land. Welcome, welcome! Now shut up! And please say something soon.
— Hot out, eh?
Not too bad yourself, my finely tanned friend. For a guy. Kevin could use some of that sun. Think he's coming up to camp tomorrow. Or tonight? Take it one minute at a time, woman. One guy at a time. One guy or a silver-haired woman? Or Jesus? Maybe I am bi. Or psychologically sacrilegious. Nice smile.
— Swimming lessons done, eh? he asks.
— Yuppers.
Just smile and pretend you didn't just say something that stupid. He's laughing. Great. Just start picking up lifejackets and hide the blush. Yuppers? Shit.
— Yuppers, eh? Nice word. Yours?

How quick is drowning? Could turn and dive off the barge pontoon. Just swim away. Probably crack my head on the pontoon and ac-tu-ally drown. Not cool not cool.
— Yeah. Like it?
— Sure. Very you.
And what you mean by that is: Very stupid, just like Maria, sayer of stupid things. And, yup, he's standing up now and ... yeah, okay, he's hot.
— What do you got next, Maria?
— Next?
— You know, after cleaning up down here.
— Hour off.
— Hangery?
Always thought that name made it sound like a parking place for planes. Apparently it's because that's where the staff *hangs*. Get it, Maria? Hangery ... hahaha ... jeez.
— Yeah, sure.
— See you there, he says. And cue the cute bum walking past me. Look the other way, straighten funny-looking fisherman's hat that keeps my nose from burning, breathe, roll daydream-of-boy ... first time in seven months.

Don't know why the telephone pole at the corner of the cookery makes me think of a cross and Kevin and how my boyfriend wants to hump me horse-like on weekends out at the old barn and still become a Catholic priest, but it does. Sometimes I kick stones here and don't look up at the hydro pole. But it's a conscious effort. And the stones themselves speak of him and that night we did it on the beach, his knees on the towel, my back scraping against the gravely sand. Just breathe heavy, like a Pentecostal, look at the stars over his shoulder, wait for one to fall and wish for something better. But it's cloudy. *Was* cloudy: past tense. Get it out of your head, woman. And don't walk into the hangery door like yesterday. Turn knob, push door, then enter.

— Bill?
— In the alcove.

Behind the curtain in the corner. His little camping trip prep room. Inner sanctum stuff. Holy of camping trip holies. And ... it's a mess. Papers all over the floor. And a big map of Algonquin Park spread out on the carpet, with amoeba-shaped circles of blue and pink highlighter.

— Pink?
— Eh?
— You use pink highlighter?
— Yeah. Why?
— Just a girly colour is all. And you're kind of like the man's man.

And he's looking at you as if you just pulled down your pants and said, Look! Ever seen the moon in the middle of the day? Probably thinking, Oh yeah, well it takes a man secure in his sexuality to be able to use pink. Keep telling yourself that, Billy-o. I do, I can see him saying it now. Every day. Sometimes I chant it to myself before I use the pink highlighter: this doesn't mean you're gay, this doesn't mean you're gay. Probably not queer-friendly, this one.

— Using pink don't mean I'm gay, eh?

He's showing me his attic, and I smell a few skeletons. That's okay. Just lock mine up tight, swallow the key and pray he doesn't slip me any verbal laxative.

— It's a joke, eh?

— Maybe.

— I piss you off?

Shrug it off and quit pouting. Where men in plaid multiply, ignorance abounds.

— Nice shirt. And, no, you didn't piss me off. I'm just touchy. Jokes like that are probably pretty common up here but they're not funny in the city.

— Up here?

— You know, hick country.

Now *he* looks pissed. He's not looking at me, picks up his clipboard: an orange whistle tied to it. Starts scribbling. What did I say? He's probably just touchy. Touchy? Like what kind of touchy? About what? Or should I say, Where? Eh? Winkwink nudgenudge. Think he's mad. Probably assumes I think he's a reg'lar old redneck and ignorant taboot. Well, you know what *assume* means, don't you? When you assume you make an *ass* out of *u* and *me*. Only heard that one a couple catrillion times! Change the subject! Honestly now, before the redneck lynches you. Ouch! That racist bigot upstairs wants to take her rainbow flag and charge the battlefield. But wait! Here comes the smile: white teeth the white flag of peace!

— So you still want to see this year's route, Maria?

— Sure.

— Take a seat on the couch.

The couch smells of mouldy cottage, mouse turds, and semen. That last might just be my imagination kicking the old olfactory sacks into high gear. Found one of the special needs kids in here three days ago, masturbating on this couch. Gross me out the door.

– Come on.

Patting the couch doesn't make it clean, Billyboy. Just swallow it. Gross. Sausage-flashback. Sit. And maybe burn your clothes tonight at campfire.

– You'd think the couch had cooties.

– Something like that, yeah.

– Here, he says, pointing to a blue circle, this is this year's trip.

He traces his finger quickly over lakes and down rivers, saying their names as he passes over them, but the names just float past me like bubbles. Like most of what he's saying. Until he starts talking about last year's trip and a girl named Jaz, who I vaguely remember.

– She back this year? I ask, remembering hazily the head counsellor telling us to check her shower kit for extra razor blades because she was a cutter.

– Nope. She's not.

He's silent and his chin's itching at his collarbone, at a hemp necklace. Four, no five, coloured beads and a little carved cross. Change the subject. This silence is claustrophobic.

– Where'd you get the necklace from?

– She made it for me on the second last day of the trip.

– Oh, nice.

– Not just a necklace, eh?

— What do you mean?
— It's a rosary.
— She Catholic?
— I am.

Probably not a good time to mention that I think the pope is a sexist bigot and an asshole in a fancy white hat. Sorry, Johnpolly, but you know where you can stick that gold sceptre, right?

— What's the sour look for? he asks.
— Honestly?

Don't speak your mind. Well, at least edit. Mental filter in place and go, after him, if he still wants my opinion: shit-dipped onion, anyone?

— Sure. Straight up, no ice.

He's a whisky drinker, good Catholic that he is. Bless his soul. Excuse me, Mary bless his soul, in the name of the Father, Son and Holy Haunted One. I could be a poet. Mental filter, woman!

— Well, after hearing the pope's position on gay marriage and his somewhat medieval views of women, I'd have to say that, honestly, and you asked for honesty, I think the pope's a bit of a prick. Freudian slip intended.

— I see.

Great! And apparently the filter is clogged with moth balls and bong resin! Guess the racist bigot upstairs is also an anti-papist.

— Can we chalk it up to differences? I offer weakly.
— Helluva difference there but ... guess it's not the first time my faith's been insulted.

Insulted his faith now, have I? Here comes the

pious pout. No. He's rather straight-lipped about it. He could've just said *challenged*. Okay. Change of subject, and quick, before I run this conversation straight into a rock-cut. Conversational crash-test dummy, Dummy. But what do you talk to a straight-lipped Catholic about?

— I had a wacky dream last night.

Kind of personal info to offer, but Bill seems like a tight-lipped, trustworthy dude. Stop using that word. You don't need to be cool in your own head. Split-personality syndrome, here I come: Hi, I'm Maria. Hi, I'm Maria Two. Nice to meet you, Skinny. Does he want the skinny?

— So what was this whacked-out dream?

— Oh, well, it's kind of crazy.

— We're all some kind of crazy.

Crazy Catholic, meet Maria's crazy sacrilegious wetdream. No, not that bad, but kind of guiltily erotic. And edit that last.

— I dreamt last night that Jesus was kissing me.

— Wow.

I'm on the toilet thinking a little of hemorrhoids but mostly of yesterday and how I learned never to confess to a Catholic. Show them a peek of the attic and they want to buy the whole house. Told Bill about one dream and next thing I'm laid out on the couch and Sigmund's great-grandson Billyboy is psychoanalyzing me like I'm some hysterical Dora, talking about tonguing Jesus but not in a I-wanna-get-it-on sort of way, like Kevin. And why did I drop *his* name? More fodder for the Catholic's fire. Or maybe he's making a file on me: Maria's inner demons and suggestions for exorcism.

So who's Kevin? he asked. I wanted to say, Listen, Siggy junior, Billy-o-boy, that's none of your business. But instead I spilled the beans:

My o-so-horny boyfriend who I can't figure out how to dump.

That gave Bill the holy-way-too-much-info look. But he just kept it coming with the queries. Queer-ies? Maybe not what he was expecting but I got this penchant for spilling on strangers. Like a look-at-me, look-at-me need to be noticed. Which usually leads to me making an ass of myself. But he seemed cool with the queer-ied me when I told him the Jesus dream was weird cause I hadn't dreamed of men since dating Kevin. And he asked me the deep — say it with a low throaty voice — *deeeep* question.

So what are you trying to say?

— I'm queer.

— Maria? That you, girl?

Forgot I was in a bathroom stall. Gawd there's a lot of blood on my arms. Think I said that last one out loud. Getting carried away and cutting too deep. Why'd I say it out loud? Mantra-ing the memory to make it reality maybe. Who am I? Who am I? I'm queer, queer-ied, querying? Just confused. Tired. Questioning. I need toilet paper.

— Maria?

— Shannelle?

— Yeah. What were you saying?

Your attic is an attic, an upper room. Keep it locked, woman. No one's supposed to walk through those locked doors. You've already given one Roman the lookaround, no need to invite the Africans in. Being a racist homosexual at a Christian camp probably won't be the most popular thing to fess up to. Especially to a black Baptist like Shannelle. But I already confessed to a Catholic. But that's kind of their thing, isn't it? Listening? And keeping things confidential? Hopefully. What do I do then? Lie?

— Said I'm weird.

— We all know that, Maria. But that's why we like you.

Sometimes I wonder if Shannelle has a mean bone in her body. I got a few. Got a mean looking rack of ribs. If I used honey garlic body wash, Kevin would probably eat me right up. Crazy carnivore.

— Maria, you coming down for supper?

— Be down in a minute, Shannelle.

Hear the flush, the stall door swing to, the sink, the towel ... and she's gone. Holy way to almost give yourself away! Not like it hasn't been done before though. What time is Kevin coming? Said I'd meet Bill tonight out on the jumping tower. Hope Kevin said it was tomorrow.

Bill's there on the jumping tower, his feet dangling over the edge, when I get there after cabin devos and lights-out. It's my night out. Shannelle gets to babysit the girls and make sure they don't sneak out to meet their camp boyfriends and do the dirty in the sports shed. Wonder what Bill thinks of the dirty? He says hi and asks me to have a seat, like he wants to say, Sit down and let me give you the prognosis: You're living in sin and you need to repent. Pretty narrow view there, Billy-o. But then again, I don't know if I'm right out there I'm-queer-and-I'm-here proud of it either. Either got to be gay and proud or Christian and straight in this crazy world. Unless you're United or Anglican.

— Any room for me in here? I ask.

— Yeah, right next to me. Hang your feet over the edge.

I tell him I'm scared of heights and he laughs and says, This is the wrong locale then, eh?

— I'm okay if I keep my eyes shut.

And my mouth. Probably too late for that though, thanks to this afternoon's verbal diarrhea. But I don't mind talking to Bill. At least he listens. Sometimes the silences are a little creepy though. Strange and striangulating — strangling.

— You okay then?

And he's a bonafide gentleman, and a Catholic taboot. Not like Kevin on either account. Wonder if Bill would want me if he knew I wasn't batting for the other team? The boards here are kind of rough but there are railings so we could roll around a little and not plummet thirty feet into the drink.

— So?

— So you want to clear up the gay thing, right?

Why in hell can't I be subtle? Holy foot-in-mouth disease. Wouldn't want to eat my foot right now though. Got camp foot. My toes are all dusty and brown. Gross me out the door and gag me with a size six big toe. Dust instead of ketchup, anyone? I must be verbally bulimic. Can't keep anything down. Got to puke it all over him so I can maintain my figure of being a skinny nincompoop. Why isn't he talking?

— What's up? I ask.

Be calm, cool, casual, collected. Silence is okay. Silence is okay. Break the silence, Bill, or I'll slap you till you talk sideways!

— You think there's something to clear up?
— You looking for another confession?
— I'm not looking for anything. Are you?

Smooth, Bill, smooth. Way to slide right in there with evangelical concern for my soul. Or a Catholic Hannibal Lector: cross-analyze and then chow down. Injest, digest, excrete, and everything goes down the crapper, salted with questions. You looking for something, Maria? Jesus is the answer. Well, if he's the answer why is he making out with me in my dreams?

— Maria?
— I'm not looking for anything. I am who I am.
— Like God. Right?

Don't try and trap me in theological garble gargling biblical phrases and trying to sing the catechism backwards while holding your upturned nose at me.

— You know the second half of that phrase? he asks.
— No. But I think you're going to tell me.
— I am who I am and I will be who I will be.

And God said to Moses this is Final Jeopardy and your category is Famous Twentieth Century Writers. The answer is: This writer is famous for repetitious run-on sentences like, I am who I am and I will be who I will be, because a rose is a rose is a rose is a rose.

— Sounds kind of like Gertrude Stein.
— El-Shaddai, actually.
— I was kidding.

— I know.

And I thought I was bad for driving the conversation into the swamp of awkward silences. Maybe he's just not used to a standard conversation like the ones I rev up.

— So, I know you got a point but I have no idea what it is, Bill.

— The second half: I will be who I will be or I will become who I will become.

— So?

— Don't let who you are stop you from who you can become.

So queer Maria present shouldn't stand in the way of the ghost of straight Maria yet to come? Sounds an awful lot like a postmodern *Christmas Carol* for poor queer kids who can give like Santa and save like Scrooge if they only follow the straight and narrow. Maybe this one will throw a wrench in his perfect little theological wheel.

— So what about Jesus making out with me in my dream?

That's right, you shake your head. A horny Jesus doesn't fit too well with the Apostle's Creed and Church Dogmatics. Along with all those Hail Marys punctuated piously with a few Our Fathers.

Bill mumbles, half laughing about Jesus maybe asking me something and I say it's hard to ask somebody anything when you have your tongue down their throat.

— It's strange. No two ways about it. But it wouldn't be the first time he did something whacked out or strange. Like how he talked to some medieval mystics.

I scrunch up my forehead here, trying to wrap my brain around what he's saying now about God maybe wanting to be my lover and I think: God Almighty wants to snog me? Well, that's a helluva way of putting it. But maybe ... maybe I'm asking the wrong question. Instead of wondering who I am or saying I *am* this, maybe he just wants to shush me with his finger to my lips like the other night and whisper something about becoming.

    Bill is getting up and mumbling so that I wonder if he's the voice in my head, but it's deeper by maybe a semi-tone – no, a key, a full key: I don't hear him. My head's buzzing. Not from what Bill said or what I think now maybe he didn't say but with the overwhelming desire to be asleep. To sleep. To just go to bed, lock the cabin door, crawl in my sleeping bag ... and? Dream. Dream of *him*, his scarred wasted body and letting my fingers fall in the valleys between his bones, his ribs, and pull his saggy skin into my fists like a blanket of flesh to wrap around me like his arms, his hands, his callused palms splotching my skin with blood. *His* blood. Like paint all red and sticky and tasting of strawberries and death's agonizing ecstasy until all I want to do is sleep with him, curl up next to him, and breathe silence in and out like heavy summer air muggy with love and sweat and the stink of me on him, his lips, his lips on mine and mine on him, on his, kissing him, licking, biting, chewing until I think I'm eating him: swallowing him up like a loaf of bread until my head breaks the surface tension of this vision, this cup, *his* cup, his cup overflowing onto my lap. Each drop ringing, buzzing until the silence is humming and alive with him, or are those mosquitoes? The lake is calm and the way the moon's reflected on its surface, if I blur my eyes a little, it looks like two moons, and if I tilt my head to the right it looks like the night is staring back at me, like *his* eyes: watery, blurred and bright. I turn around, expecting Bill to be waiting for me but he's gone. Not such a gentleman afterall. But as I stand I can't clear my head. Not of what Bill said but of *his* face, that ugly grotesque face and that patchy scar-scratched beard. And I want to see him again. So I start back along the trail to my cabin, my bed, *our* bed. But when I get to the clearing where the head counsellors park their cars, I see headlights pulling in and I hear Kevin's voice:

— Hey, Maria! Come on, Baby. Hop in and let's go somewhere tonight. I know it's your night off! Hey, Maria!

I just drop my head and walk past even as Kevin yells my name again and again, and each time, each time his tongue rounds the three syllables of my name, I feel his body like sandpaper against mine, trying to smooth me down and shape me into his little sex toy or plaything: his trophy. Some prize *I* am. I am. I am not what he thinks I am. I'm not what anyone thinks I am! I'm becoming something. Something other. Something ... some*one*.

— Maria! Where in hell are you going?

— To meet someone!

The door! The door. I don't even know if the door has a lock. To keep him out. To keep me in. Inside the cabin: my sleeping bag cocooning me, comforting me as I stop my ears from his voice in the night. Kevin's voice. Like a needle in my ear.

CRAFTY OLD DRAGON

Reg is taking a long draw on his cigarette, standing in the shade of his garage door, when the kitchen window of his neighbours' cottage shatters and a cast-iron skillet skids across the gravel driveway, sending Pepper – Reg's cocker spaniel – into a barking fit.

"Back at it, eh?" Reg says as he blows a smoke ring and whistles for his dog. "Pepper! You dumb-ass canine! Get back here!"

Pepper sniffs at the greasy skillet, hears Dick and Vicky – Reg's neighbours – hollering at each other through the broken window, and decides to join in with his own howling.

Reg flicks his cigarette onto the gravel driveway and heads back into the dark of his garage to the beer fridge he's got under his workbench. He'd been wondering where his nephew Ben was at. Was it B.C. or Toronto now? The boy got out of Napanee Correctional Facility early, on good behaviour. Did his parole and then took off to the West Coast to be a tree-planter. Reg used to take the kid fishing, but that was before the young lad knifed his dad.

Reg was mulling all this over before the skillet crashed through the window. He hears his dog tonguing away along with his two old neighbours as he pushes thoughts of his nephew to the back of his mind and pulls a beer from the fridge, twisting the cap off with his shirt sleeve.

He holds his beer up in a toast to the lone lightbulb over his workbench.

Reg nods to the light and says, "To Dick: grey-haired dragon tamer!" And with that he downs half his beer. Occasionally Dick will join him in drinking, but Reg is pretty sure that Dick spends most of his time battling his wife – the Dragon – over everything from mowing the lawn to putting in the dock, bailing out the boat, drinking too much or leaving tools all over the kitchen counter.

Reg whistles once more for Pepper and the old cocker spaniel saunters in, sits, and looks up, panting at him. Reg glances down at his dog, pulls out another cigarette, lights it and slowly blows smoke out his nostrils. He can hear Dick giving a long address comprising mostly short, one-syllabled, four-lettered words to Vicky; halfway through which Vicky joins in. Their argument crescendos until, suddenly, everything goes eerily silent.

Reg looks out the garage door and over the lake, across the dirt road from his cottage, and he sees the heat glistening on the still, tepid, late-August water. He exhales another puff of smoke that mushrooms above his head.

"Boom!" he says quietly as he looks at his dog, rolls his

eyes, and turns back to his workbench to find the tools to finish tweaking the bilge system on his new bass boat.

Dick is standing in front of the sink, his back to the broken window, looking at the shards of glass on the floor. He glances over his shoulder at the kitchen counter and looks up through the broken window, imagining Vicky's cow-sized behind mounted there to block the wind. He sees more broken glass. The Welch's frozen grape juice container he uses for a spittoon is on its side and brown tobacco spit is creeping across the counter, weaving its way through the archipelago of shattered glass.

He reaches into the breast pocket of his green work shirt, unbuttoned to his chest, and pulls out a roll of Lifesavers and a can of Copenhagen chewing tobacco. He pops the Lifesavers back into his pocket – they're for his grandkids when they pull on his belt and ask "Grampa" for a twiddle – and he takes a pinch of tobacco, wads it into his lower lip, screws the cap back on the container and re-pockets the Copenhagen while scanning what the Dragon has laid waste to this time.

They're down two glasses and a mug – Vicky threw those at him before her hand found the frying pan – and she kicked the garbage can over as her last exclamation point. Vicky knows punctuation and she's pretty creative with her grammar too; she can use the f-bomb as any part of speech – adjective, noun, verb, coordinating conjunction – whereas Dick doesn't get much beyond using it in an adjectival barrage, though he wouldn't know to call it that himself.

Well, he thinks as he runs his hand over his bald head

and scratches his wrinkly neck, if she thinks I'm cleaning up after her tirade she's vastly mistaken.

So he shuffles out of the kitchen, grabbing the box of soda biscuits off the counter, and heads around the woodstove to the table. He seats himself in his chair, his back to the eight-track/record player and the black rotary phone, and proceeds to lay out ten crackers in a row on the table in front of him. He blows some air through his lips, puffs out his cheeks, and exhales, tasting heartburn and coffee.

He listens for any movement from upstairs – Vicky's cave, where she goes to lick her wounds after a fight – but he doesn't hear anything except the tick-tick-ticking of the grandfather clock in the living room.

His eyes fall to his ten soda biscuits and he starts counting their holes when he hears a squirrel scold from the maple tree that overshadows the porch. He looks out the screen door to the porch swing he built for Vicky last year after they had a big blow-out in front of their daughter Reece over shit stains in his long underwear. He'd been pretty embarrassed and he tore a thick strip off Vicky for mentioning it. Afterwards he'd felt like a complete, castrated ass and he wanted to make it up to Vicky, but his pride was a fishbone he couldn't swallow – so he built her a swing instead.

She loved the swing and she'd sit on it for hours in the evenings, listening to the loons out on Lemming's Lake in the summer, and in June, when the Pentecostal church on the island was having their outdoor camp meetings, she'd hum the old spirituals and hymns that moved audibly but unseen in the summer air like spirits.

Dick looks from the swing to the porch he'd promised to sand and re-stain in May, and then back to the swing, remembering how Vicky had been curled up and sleeping on it one day when the rope on the one side busted and sent her rolling across the deck like a large, fleshy rolling pin.

Did he ever howl over that one!

Dick smiles at the memory, pops out his dentures and inserts a cracker, which he lets dissolve in his mouth – the salt mingling with the bitter tobacco juice. He looks around for a can or cup to use for a spittoon and is about to hork a mouthful over the kitchen counter onto the glass-covered floor – for Vicky to clean up later – when he hears movement upstairs. He holds the tobacco spit in his mouth and looks into the living room at the stairs against the far wall.

He's let down his guard and now the Dragon is stirring again: coming for round two! The first go at it he can hold his own, but round two is when Vicky spits the snakefire she's been brewing upstairs – round two is the intellectual bout, and Vicky has Dick beat in that category.

This part actually scares him a bit.

So he starts looking for a knife. Not a sharp one: just a butter knife, so he can spread peanut butter on his crackers and act like he's busy when she comes into the room.

He can't find a clean one so he pulls a dirty one out of a cold, half-full cup of coffee left over from breakfast. He wipes it nervously on his pant leg, trying to find his breastplate of anger, his shield of sarcasm, and his sword of smart-ass quips among the dirty dishes, salt and pepper shakers, and condiments on the table in front of him.

But he can't find them anywhere nearby so he spreads

his crackers with peanut butter and reaches for a can of sardines, hearing the Dragon's bulk creak the floorboards of their bedroom as she moves towards the stairs! Vicky hates the smell of sardines, Dick thinks as he fiddles with the can, trying to get it open with his nervous, twitching fingers.

He's convinced after forty-odd years that pissing her off is his only defense.

"Calm down!" he mumbles to himself. "This isn't the first time you've rubbed her scales the wrong way and got yer nose hairs torched!" But as much as he tries he can't calm himself. He can't get his heart to stop two-stepping around inside his chest. He can't stop his fingers from twitching.

And he can't get the friggin lid off the sardine can! So he reefs one last time on the little metal tab and the lid peels back, spilling stinking fish juice all over his lap.

"Judas H. Priest!" he gurgles through a mouthful of tobacco juice as he starts wiping his pants with a tea towel. But he freezes again when he hears the first stair creak.

He reaches for a fork that's still pierced through a piece of breakfast sausage and starts fishing the sardines out of the can and onto the soda biscuits.

By the time he has the crackers spread and seafood-garnished, Vicky is on the last step. He can see her purple slacks and swollen, blue-veined feet in cheap, dirty-white Wal-Mart slippers as she steps into the living room.

Dick grips the fork in his right hand and scoops up a cracker in his left; he sees Vicky cross the living room with deliberate steps, like a haggard old god striding towards her judgment seat. And when she reaches the doorway to the dining room Dick stuffs the cracker into his mouth, forgetting about the swig of tobacco juice stewing behind his lips.

Brown spit dribbles down Dick's unshaven, stubbly chin as he faces the Dragon with his cheeks puffed out like a greedy chipmunk. Everything in Dick's body tells him to spew but when Vicky takes another step towards him he swallows.

His face immediately blanches white and he feels the gears in his stomach flipping to reverse. But he swallows hard and blinks away a few tears as he watches the Dragon puff herself up, he thinks, to belch sulphur and spit brimstone.

But Vicky just lets out a deep sigh, lets her eyes drop to the cracked linoleum floor, and walks over to where the broom stands behind the door.

Dick watches her begin to sweep the spilled contents of the garbage can back into it and turn it upright. He watches her begin to sweep up the glass near the kitchen sink. He feels sick to his stomach. He stands to his feet and stumbles to the screen door, pulls it open, and staggers out onto the porch.

When he reaches the railing he wants to hurl but he can't. He feels his stomach gurgle. A shudder passes through him. And he suddenly feels cold, his skin clammy. He hasn't felt like this since he helped pull Jim's body out of the lake after Jim drowned in a boating accident while fishing with Dick's grandson Christopher. That wasn't too long ago, either. A year maybe.

He shakes his head to try and clear his mind of that dark recollection but he just makes himself dizzy and has to hold onto the porch railing. He spits over the edge and tries to swallow again. Finally, he looks up, squints against the sun, pulls out a Lifesaver and pops it in his mouth. He remembers the little jingle he sings to his grandkids: Twiddle twiddle, it's the only candy with the hole in the middle, twiddle twiddle.

He spits again, and then lifts his eyes to the hills across the lake and behind the island, beyond the steeple of the Pentecostal church – feeling Jim's ghost drift away from him into the shadows of the trees. He looks across the lake to the spot where the sun will set come evening. And he smiles. Even though his lips don't show it, his blue eyes are glistening because he knows something – a small revelation like a spark in his head.

He knows that he's going to turn around, walk inside, and help Vicky clean up their mess. He knows he's going to apologize – perhaps for the first time, verbally, in forty years – for that comment he made about Vicky's sister Stella. He knows he's going to say, "Mmmm ... tasty," when she makes him side pork, mashed potatoes and grease gravy for supper, because that's her way of apologizing. And he knows he'll sit beside her on the swing tonight and he'll whittle away on a stick with his jack-knife while she listens to the loons. And after they've tired of watching mosquitoes burn to death in the bug zapper – around 9:30 pm – he'll follow her to bed and let her fall asleep first so he doesn't keep her up with his snoring.

Reg sees Dick walk back into his cottage. He looks down at Pepper, who is sitting, panting at his feet. He takes a swig of his seventh beer and walks a little drunkenly back into his garage where he pours the rest of the beer into Pepper's dog dish and reaches for the rotary phone hanging on the wall over his workbench.

He dials Dick's number and prays to Saint Joseph that Vicky doesn't pick up.

"Hello," he hears Dick's voice on the other end.

"Hello, Dick. Reg here."

"Hey, Reg."

"You up for a fish tonight?"

"No, Reg. Not tonight."

"No, eh?" Reg mutters in the phone, thinking, *the Dragon's cast her guilt-spell!*

"Gotta go, Reg. Talk to you tomorrow."

Reg hears the click and the dial tone. He hangs up, shakes his head and walks out into the afternoon sunlight. Pepper hears something down by the water and dashes across the dirt road and disappears over the embankment. Reg hears a splash and wonders if Pepper is chasing a water snake or pawing at crayfish this time, or a school of minnows.

Poor Dick, he thinks as he puts his hands on his back and cracks his lower spine. *He got eaten by the Dragon again. And the hell of it is, I think in some twisted way he likes getting chewed out by her.*

Crafty old dragon, that one.

ROULETTE

"God!"

I sit up straight in my bed, not sure if this bark of a prayer was in my head or yelled aloud. The silence around me congeals and smells of bacon fat – my apartment. I must've screamed in my head. My breathing is heavy: congested, like my Uncle Reg's breathing that rattles the tar in his chest cause he's smoked half a carton a day since he was twelve.

I didn't start smoking until the nightmares started.

My eyes dart around in the dark as I try to bring the familiar objects that surround me into focus – pupils dilating until I recognize the black rotary phone on the floor by the bed, the bare unpainted drywall splotched with water stains, a handgun on my sheetless mattress beside my pillow, which is a couch cushion wrapped in a T-shirt.

You're okay, I tell myself, it was just a nightmare.

A nightmare that's driving me to insomnia.

I look over at the tattered paperback novel of that name,

by Stephen King. I bought it at the drugstore when I was picking up my prescription for Tylenol 3, wanting to read something to remind me that I'm not the only sorry hick who can't sleep.

I flick on the light next to my bed and collapse on my back. There's a sopping sound. My mattress is soaked. I look to the ceiling that is warped and stained from leaks, but when I sit up and look to the window over my shoulder I see it's not raining.

It's sweat.

My whole body is soaked and my skin is clammy. I run my hand over my face, wipe it on the mattress that creaks under me, and then scratch the back of my head, fingering scar tissue.

I'll have to get a new mattress soon. There's a Salvation Army store not far from here. This one smells of sweat and piss. My feet touch the cold wood floor. I drop my hand from my neck and finger my crotch.

Wet again.

I'm twenty-five and still piss the bed.

I try to stand. The cold floor makes my feet ache. A flash of pain splits the blackness in my head.

I'm back in the nightmare. Surrounded by trees. And running. Lead legs melting and becoming wax in the half-frozen spruce swamp. I hear two breaths panting. My heart pounds. It's closing in on me. There's no way to go. Even if there was I can't because my only escape is barred. Terror a hot wet roar—

My eyes snap open. I'm in my room. My apartment near the railroad tracks. The unfinished walls warped and sagging like the damp nylon walls of a tent in the rain — like the tent

I lived in, out in B.C., working as a tree-planter, after they let me out of Napanee. When I knew I couldn't go home. Before the bear hunt.

My hand is on the revolver.

But it's over.

I'm awake.

And it isn't raining.

Let it go. Don't mull on it, I tell myself. But the nightmare's as real as that metal pipe just under the snow when I was a kid and sledding down the hill between Uncle Reg's cottage and Dick's house and fell off my sled and slit the skin from the back of my knee to my arse crack.

The nightmare makes me bleed sometimes.

Because I don't have anything to cut my fingernails that puncture the skin of my palms when I clench my fists against the pain.

It's that real – the nightmare. All of them. But it's in the past.

I tell myself not to think about it.

But it's there every time I close my eyes.

My eyelids are heavy and dry. I keep on opening and closing them, trying to squeeze out tears, but it's too cold. Sometimes in the winter tears freeze halfway down my face as I sit on the corner by the Tim Hortons with my hat on the pavement, weighted down with pennies.

Got to make rent somehow.

It's best to pocket the loonies and bills. Or else people stop giving. They give more in the winter too. Playing homeless from November to February is better than working a nine to fiver. Cause of the cold and snow people feel sorry for you. Though it's never really cold here in the city. Not like back home.

Not like that night when I was fifteen and got lost in the bush in a snowstorm after I stabbed my father with his own hunting knife and left him to bleed on the kitchen floor. I'd stumbled through the bush with nothing but a tattered jack-shirt on for warmth and broke through the ice on the swamp near Frank's brother's house. Only up to my waist though. And I was able to pull myself out because of a spruce tree growing sideways out of the bank, over the ice. Like a giant arm reaching over me. I pulled myself out of the swamp and flopped over that branch to catch my breath. But I fell asleep in the cold and would've froze there if my mom hadn't found my dad's body and called the police and Dan – God knows why she phoned a seventy-five-year-old man with a bad hip – and Dan tracked me from the house, through the bush and to the swamp, where he found me hung over that branch.

I shiver at the memory. Of coming to in the bathtub in Frank's brother's house – can't remember his name. Just know Frank's name cause it was in the *Bancroft Times* after he got gutted on a ripsaw at the mill. Paper didn't put it that way but that's the bones of it. And I was in his brother's tub, in his brother's house, when I came to: shivering, teeth chattering, and his two young lads staring at me cause their tub was in their living room.

Heard the one young lad got killed a while back.

News gets to me even here.

They know I'm alive.

Dan knows. And my mom. She sends me a package

every month full of old *Daily Bread* devotionals and the *Bancroft Times*. I use the devotional booklets for rolling papers. I read them beforehand, and then smoke them. Sometimes I wave the cigarette around like an altar boy swings the urn of incense during mass. Or is that the priest? I was an altar boy once. Before Dad broke the priest's teeth and Mom started going to the Pentecostal church cause she was embarrassed and scared. I was an altar boy for two years. Now I use scripture to roll my cigarettes. Sometimes I think I'm blaspheming but other times I breathe in the smoke and think, maybe I'm inhaling Him, the big J. Seems that salvation enters you through the mouth. He's in the wafers, they say, and the incense. The priest said He's everywhere so why not here?

I read the highlighted stories in the *Bancroft Times* while I smoke. Mom highlights certain stories – like that kid's death and how Dillan Witaker's boy killed a professor at the University of Toronto cause he OD'ed on some bad shit.

I've tried it. The hard stuff. Powder mostly.

Snorted lines of it one day trying to kill the pain. But all it did was release the beast from my nightmares into the daylight and send me screaming around my apartment, too strung out to load the handgun. Or that would've been the end of it.

Sometimes I wish I'd pre-loaded the gun. Left the single shell in the chamber.

But I didn't.

And I've regretted not having the foresight ever since cause I don't actually have the guts to pull the trigger. Too many sermons on suicide when I was a kid and my grandma dragged me and my mom to mass. I want to die but I'm afraid of hell cause there's no waking from it.

My hands are shaking.

I need some coffee.

I remember my dad telling me of when he did shift work in the old days at the mill. He and the guys would start their shift on Friday night and get off on Monday morning. During those weekend marathons they would drink pots of coffee to maintain their zombie-like state of semi-proficiency. Dad used to say that by those Monday mornings the pains in his chest would be so bad he felt like someone was tearing his ribs loose.

That's how I feel now. But I'll put up with chemicals, mangling my body if they keep me away from that place. Remembering my father is better than remembering the other. That place where I live the whole thing over again.

Old scars burn with new fire.

I stumble to the kitchen. Pots are strewn about the counter that's speckled with spaghetti sauce. The sink isn't full but that's just because I only own three dishes and one set of cutlery. A lot of pots though.

In the proliferation of pots I find my kettle. I fill it from the tap and set it to boil on the glowing element, thinking "proliferation" is a friggin queer word and I don't know why I know it or think it when I look at the mess on my counter, except that I might've read it in the paper once and liked the way my tongue rolled over it.

I look around for something to do. There was something I was going to do. I've already filled the kettle and put it on to boil.

THIS RAMSHACKLE TABERNACLE

I collapse onto the only chair in the kitchen. Close my eyes and wait to hear the kettle sing when its bolt — that's how we say "boiled" back home, even though it's not my home and I haven't been back since being sent to Napanee after knifing my dad.

Home.

The word's like a kiss. Like how I imagine a kiss to be: lips puckered and droning the "m" like how I'd say "mmmm" when Mom would serve up turkey soup made from boiling the carcass left over from the church pot-lock, which she'd cabbage each year at Christmas time.

Turkey soup and tea. No sugar for tea. No salt for the soup. But pepper. Always black pepper that Dad would steal from Dan's corner store. "He'd miss the salt," Dad would say, smiling and chuckling to himself, "but nobody misses pepper!"

And he was right.

At least I think he was right.

Or maybe Dan would've given us salt if we'd asked. But Dad was too proud. Too proud and too mean. That's why I stuck him with the knife. Cause he was too proud to apologise for hitting Mom and me. Too mean to stop.

So I stuck him. Between the ribs. Heard his breath whistle from him.

I can hear him now, wheezing.

Whistling a high-pitched scream.

But it's not him; it's the kettle — water's bolt.

The pain in my ear from the high-pitched whistle fuses with the numbness of my shoulder. The kickback of the rifle.

The gun is empty.

No.

Jammed.

The shell won't load and my .308 is useless in my shaking hands.

I look up into its black eyes. Straight down the grizzly's gaping maw.

Fight a black bear.

Flee a grizzly.

Flee?

Where in hell to?

No place to go but down the gaping jaws that open to roar in my face. The sound shakes my bowels loose and I shit myself.

I drop to my knees in a dead faint.

Unconscious.

Nearly.

But I can still feel it flay me from ankles to ears with talons that catch and tear at every nerve. I'm a bleeding lump of raw meat, which it rolls and rolls in pine needles. Grizzlies play with their food. That's what they said when we started up with the tree-planting company in B.C.

But that was on the West Coast. A few years ago. After months in the hospital. Before I used the last of my money to buy a backpack and hitchhiked back to Ontario. I had to carry my bag cause I couldn't stand to have it on my back, even though the wounds had healed.

Scar-tissue stings still.

I blink and realize I must've sunk into the nightmare while awake. Least I think I'm awake. The sun shines through the criss-crossing of pine needles. I free myself from my would-be jackpine shroud and stand there, an open, seeping piece of flesh. The sun is dark and blue is red as I stumble colour-blinded by pain out of the throat-like canyon.

I hear the roar of a truck.

Where's the bear?

The sound of the truck escalates to a high-pitched whistle-like scream and I cover my ears and run tripping and banging into things, yelling madly and scrambling for the gun – the handgun – and wheel around, cocking it and aiming blindly at the scream of my father that slides down octaves like blood off my fingers till it's a roar that causes me to squeeze the trigger–

Silence.

Except for dripping.

Blood on linoleum.

Boiling water hissing on the hot stove-top – the element on high – and hot water dripping onto the floor: the unsanded plywood floor that squeaks like the springs of my bed.

There's a bullet hole through the kettle and I hear screaming from the far side of the wall in the next apartment. It's Chinese, I think, or maybe Korean. There's a Korean Presbyterian church nearby. But these people don't go to church. They yell at each other on Sunday mornings.

The water pops and fizzles on the hot element. The boiling water drips down the rusted front of the stove. My kettle has a hole in it. A bullet hole. I had one bullet in that gun.

"Why do you want a handgun?" the shifty guy asked me when I bought it.

The scar tissue on my back and neck – all the way down

to my ankles – burned in the early wet winter cold. "Why?" I asked him back.

"Why not go to a gunshop? Get it legal?"

"I got a record."

"Prison?"

"Juvie."

"You part of a gang?"

"I hunt."

"What do you hunt?"

My scars burned like when my dad poured scalding tea down the back of my shirt: each nerve in my skin writhing and screaming like leeches in the fire. I was on Tylenol 3 but painkillers didn't do anything. They only made me tired, so I'd fall asleep – into that ravine.

With it.

I looked at the guy. "I hunt grizzlies."

"Handgun's no good against a bear."

"The gun's not for the bear," I said and lifted the back of my shirt to show him the deepest scar that ran from my hipbone to my first rib, along the spine. The thing could have deboned me like I used to debone trout roasted over the coals of a campfire.

"You get mauled?" the guy asked, his face green.

I didn't answer. I just tucked my shirt back into my pants. Picked up the revolver off the lid of the trash can. And the one shell. I think it was one shell – maybe two. Said that's all I needed. I handed over the money in bills and small change.

Now I hear the occasional drip. The screaming next door has stopped. I step forward and see that the bullet is lodged in the back of the stove. The water has stopped running out of the kettle, onto the hot element and onto the plywood floor. The kettle's empty. Now I don't have a kettle. And I can't make coffee.

Or shoot myself, for that matter.

I hear sirens coming down the street. Sirens like kettles boiling on hot elements.

I sit on the bed with the gun in my right hand. Shaking my head and making the bed springs squeak. The bed squeaks but I can still hear boots striking against the stairs as red and blue lights flash through my curtainless window.

The cops are outside my door.

There is silence like spit on the floor.

Like hot water dripping.

The silence hisses like water on the hot element.

And I start to laugh. They break down the door and I'm laughing, laughing so hard I crack my teeth on the barrel of the gun that's in my mouth. Laughing so hard tears run down my face as I pull the trigger again and again and—

THE KILLING TREE

They call it the killing tree. A few years ago its boughs were heavy with apple blossoms in the spring, and fist-sized MacIntoshes in the early fall. But wormwood took it at the core and squeezed the sap out until its branches were brittle and leafless. It died soon after they found Garret hanging from the noose. I was away at university in Toronto when it happened, learning how to swim in an undergraduate creative writing seminar; word of Garret's suicide was like a large rock hurled my way.

"Bill," my mom had said over the phone, "you should come home. It's Garret. He's ... he ..."

That phone call was three years ago a week this Wednesday.

Winter.

Maybe it was the February weather that did it. There had been no sun since January 28th of that year. Maybe the dank half-dark soaked through his jacket and snuffed out the embers of hope. I saw them burn from black to orange when he inhaled. Sometimes I would watch him draw with pursed lips on the end of a joint and then stare at the burning end, holding the smoke inside, until his eyes watered or the joint burned down to scorch his fingers. He smoked up out by the apple tree in the field behind his house or in the fish hut he built wigwam-style out of pine boughs out on Spruce Lake, near the hunting camp.

He'd drive out to the lake on his 1973 skidoo. The writing on the hood had peeled off with the finish. The seat's upholstery had been replaced with innumerable duct-tape patches and the runner boards were rusting away. But he drove the snot out of that thing, flying down the sled trail to the lake. Once he crashed into a poplar tree and busted off one of the skis.

He kept the thing going though, even after the snow had melted in the spring; he'd fly down the Ridge Road, engine snarling and gravel catching in the bogies and spinning out sideways like gunshots.

Freda, the crazy feminist redneck who lives in the shack next to Jack Skreef's place, saw Garret roaring up the road on his skidoo one day in July when she was re-shingling her roof in the buff. When he ripped past her house, she heaved the hammer at him but missed the sled by a hand. When Garret came back down the road she was standing by the ditch, naked as Eve, except for her tool belt and a mesh-backed Husqvarna hat turned backwards on her head. She flipped him the bird when he buzzed by, but she got pelted by the spray of dirt and gravel.

I laughed pretty hard when I heard that.

Kind of makes me smile now, too. But standing knee-deep in snow under the killing tree brings me back to the fact that Garret's not here anymore, and his sled is rusting away behind his parents' house, back behind the dead-stock barn where his dad used to grind up dead animals that farmers paid him to dispose of. Some became fertilizer, some dog food, but most went to feeding his dad's minks, which would get skinned each year, and the pelts sold to a fur trader near Bancroft.

Back in the summer, when Garret was a kid, Jack Skreef, who lived across the road, would stack up brush, raked from around his farm, and hold a big bonfire and invite the whole community. At those gatherings, Garret would play with me and Sean and Sean's little brother Wes. The four of us would hunt through the forest and find branches to throw on the flames. Jack usually had a pile of junk to throw on the blaze from a barn he'd demolished with his bulldozer — because he ran his own demolition business — but that was always done by the adults.

The men.

Garret had tried to help once, but he stepped on a nail that went right through his foot. His dad slapped the side of his head seven or eight times on the way into Bancroft to the hospital, but when the nurses asked about the bruising on the back of his head Garret's dad said it was because the boy fell out of a barn loft and they should check for concussion. He'd whispered something to Garret then, before they took him in. After that, they couldn't get Garret to say anything: not one word to their many questions.

"So how are you today, Garret?"

"Does the nail hurt?"

"Do you want anything for the pain?"

"Do you know if you've had a recent tetanus shot?"

Not one word. Not one flinch, even when they pulled the nail out and blood flowed onto the white sheet. Not even when they sent him home the next day with his foot swollen to twice the size of the other one.

His dad had joked with him on the way back to St. Lola.

"You're lucky, eh?"

He looked at his dad as if to ask: Why?

"You'll have a Jesus scar from that one. That's gotta be good luck, right? Eh?"

Garret just shrugged and leaned away from his dad, against the window of the old Chevy truck that roared too loudly down Highway 62 because its muffler was rusted away.

One time, at another bonfire several summers later, Garret took me and Sean and Wes across the road from Jack Skreef's and into his dad's dead-stock barn to show us the rotten carcass of a cow that had lain dead in a field for a week in the July heat before it was found. He had us gather around the dead cow, its stomach bloated and distended with putrefaction, and said, "Tadaa!" hitting the side of the cow with a crowbar, splitting the skin open, and letting a slimy ball of maggots spill out onto the cement floor along with the cow's rotten intestines. The smell made the rest of us vomit and run back to our mothers crying.

Garret laughed, even while his dad beat him with the buckle end of his belt that night, after polishing off a bottle of whisky and half a case of Coke.

Garret would take those beatings with a smirk on his face and then run out of the house, through the dead-stock barn, and out to the apple tree, which he'd climb up into and not answer his mother's calls for supper or his dad's threats about getting his ass in the house before nightfall – hidden away in the thick green foliage.

Now patches of bark still cling to the tree, but much of the trunk is bare and drilled with woodpecker holes. Termite trails snake up from the roots.

I'm standing under the branch that held the rope he hung himself from.

My feet are cold and they hurt. My back hurts too, from falling on the icy drive coming in. I always seemed to be falling when I was around Garret. Like that time we were jumping in the haymow and it was the December he was ten and he fell through the open trap door and reached out for a hand and pulled me down with him so that we spun in the air, and I landed in a pile of hay while he landed on the frozen floorboards that cracked under his little knees. I remember him limping from the barn into the house, crying.

As he grew up, though, he stopped crying because his dad would whip him more if he cried; so he stopped to spite his dad – to challenge him. It wasn't until grade ten that he heard that his dad had been terrorized as a kid by guys his own his age who lived on the Ridge Road: kids who grew up to be his neighbours. Apparently, back when Garret's grandfather ran the dead-stock farm, Ziggy and Jim Carrol grabbed Garret's dad by his ankles and stuck him headfirst in a barrel of sheep intestines and goat's blood. When Garret heard that story from his mom he stopped trying to egg his dad on and started spending more time in the bush trying to grow his own marijuana.

But he could never seem to get it to grow in the rocky soil out back of his house, anymore than anyone could get anything to grow up on the Ridge, where there were ten farms and no crops.

So he had to buy his stash from a dealer at school who was rumoured to have sold some to his friend Sean for a blow job. But he didn't think that was true and he'd fight anyone who said otherwise – especially after Sean died. He once beat a rugby player senseless – one of the guys who was said to have been responsible for his friend's death – until the kid, who was twice his size and two grades ahead, lay motionless on the road out behind the high school, blood running out of his nose and mouth.

He'd been suspended for that fight and for three others like it.

When his dad heard, he beat him with a tire iron until he'd broken Garret's arm, and his mom had called the police and had his dad arrested. Social services got involved in the prosecution and somehow, with his history of abuse, he got attempted murder. That got him shipped off to Kingston Penitentiary.

Garret never went to see him: his dad. Never went to the prison with his mom. He didn't say anything when she told him that his dad was starting AA in prison and was going through rehab. Apparently his dad started in on that after he'd seen another prisoner murdered in the showers.

Sometimes I'd walk with Garret when he'd trudge through the snow out into the fields, or back through the trails to Spruce Lake, or to the old apple tree – during those long nights his mom would be away visiting his dad.

Somebody told me Garret's dad shared a cell with Ben LeBou, Reg Hughes' nephew, who stabbed his own dad a few years back. I know now that Ben was in Napanee not Kingston. He got out a year before Garret's dad. I've heard that Ben went tree-planting in B.C. after he'd finished his parole. Got mauled by a grizzly but survived somehow and is living in Toronto, last I heard. Garret's mom would give us snippets of information like this as the three of us sat about their kitchen table, sipping tea from chinked mugs, the conversation consisting largely of thick silences.

Then, on one of those days Garret's mom was away, one of those damp cold days when you can feel winter about to give out but you know it's still hanging on, its icy claws dug deep into the earth – on that February day three years back a week ago this Wednesday, it happened.

In my mind I follow Garret out to the apple tree and I climb up into it with him, and sit there as visible, yet unnoticed, as the snow on the branches.

As I'm standing here now I recall the wind that day – wet and bitter.

I imagine Garret seating himself astride the thick branch while he ties the rope around it three times before knotting it to hold. His long, greasy black hair hangs about his face as he wraps the end of the rope around and around before sliding it through to hold the noose in place. Then he puts the rope over his head like a necktie and lights a joint as he leans back against the tree trunk. He closes his eyes as he inhales and holds the smoke inside him until his head begins to nod.

Then he just falls out of the tree.

I see myself climb down and pick up the half-smoked joint that has fallen and gone out. A fatty: the last of his stash. I imagine rolling the joint back and forth between my thumb and forefinger as I stare at the tree.

The tears freeze in my eyes – an icy veneer. Garret's image is blurred and distorted in my mind, like I'm looking at him from under the ice of Spruce Lake.

I'm standing in the same spot now, looking up to where Garret hung like a marionette on a string. My feet are cold as I stand in the wet snow, imagining Garret's heavy steps as he pushed through the snow and cold on his way to his gallows.

As I stand in the golgothic shadow of the killing tree I hear, in the dead -20 degree air, the chirping of a cardinal singing its wintersong from the topmost branch.

At the sound I look up to the pine-forested hills. The setting sun sketches contours of crimson on the clouded February sky – a kind of divine chiaroscuro, maybe. That's the way I think. Once a Catholic, always a Catholic. Maybe this is how God bleeds himself into the world: with the coming of night and darkness. Incarnate long before the sun rises. Sometimes I feel like I'm still waiting for the sun to rise: like it hasn't really risen these past three years. Wondering, if God's hand is there in the dark why doesn't he reach out and touch us?

There are rumours that Garret's dad is coming home soon – sober, but too late. He's already asked Jack Skreef to cut down the killing tree with his chainsaw and chop it up with his woodsplitter. He's planning on having a huge bonfire and inviting the whole community. He hopes they'll all come – not for his sake, but for Garret.

He's planning on dousing the bones of the killing tree in diesel fuel and setting them ablaze and burning Garret's snowmobile along with the tree his boy hung himself from. And, though he hasn't said this to anyone, I imagine he'd allow himself to be submerged in a barrel of sheep's blood again and run screaming into the midst of the bonfire if he thought it'd bring his son back.

SHEKINAH

"She looked right at me and said it was a clichéd story about drug addiction," Bill said as he crunched through the November snow behind his Uncle Ziggy.

"She said that? Girl in yer workshop?" Ziggy asked as they approached the dead deer lying on its side.

"Yeah." Bill scratched his orange toque and remembered the girl telling him how cartooned his characters were: how real characters didn't scratch their heads like monkeys. "Said the story didn't do it for her."

"What?" Ziggy quipped as he handed his 30/30 Winchester to Bill and pulled out his hunting knife. "She expect your story to be a friggin vibrator?"

Bill snorted a laugh and had to wipe the snot from his mustache. "You got a queer way of putting things," he chuckled, thinking about how his classmates at university would skin him for using that expression, though he'd used it long before he'd ever heard of homosexuality.

"That the story about the Witaker boy?"

"Yeah."

"Hmph," Ziggy grunted as he bent over. "You wanna stick it to her?" he asked as he plunged the hunting knife into the deer's soft white-furred underbelly.

Bill thought about the question as he watched his uncle saw the knife blade in and out of the deer, spilling blood on the snow as he opened up the stomach. He remembered the cold feeling in his chest when the girl had ripped into his story, telling him it was nothing new, that he was repeating himself and the story just simply didn't work. He watched Ziggy reach both his bare hands into the deer's open belly and haul out a pile of guts that steamed in the frosty air.

"Eh?" Ziggy looked over his shoulder at his nephew, raised an eyebrow because Bill was just staring at him – the Winchester in one hand and the young lad's shotgun slung over a shoulder. "Snap out of it, eh."

Ziggy shook his woolly head and wiped his bloodied hands on the snow. He picked up his knife, walked over to the deer's head and started screwing the tip of the knife into one of the nostrils. "People will always tag ya, eh?" He smiled as he reached into his pocket and pulled out his doe tag. "See?" He laughed at his joke and then worked the wire of the tag up one nostril, through the hole he'd made into the other nostril, and then out again, where he pasted the paper ends over the wires. "There!" he spit as he hauled himself to his feet.

"Beauty," Bill said as he looked at the corpse of the deer, its stomach slit open and its intestines lying in a steaming heap near its hooves. The snow was red all around the deer's body. He glanced at the doe's head, cranked backwards at a sharp angle, blood leaking out its nose, staining the white paper of the tag: the snow. "Nice." He smiled, feeling at peace for some reason, as if the shedding of blood had made everything right in his world, even if just for that moment.

"She's a beaut, eh?" Dan said as he stood beside Bill by the front door of the hunting cabin, looking at the body of the deer hanging with a chain wrapped around its rear legs from the branch of a white pine. "Ziggy's a crack shot, I'll tell you." Dan clapped a big wrinkled old hand down on Bill's shoulder before heading into the cabin. Bill thought of the story he'd written about Dan, based on a walk they'd taken out on the Crossroads near St. Olga, when Dan had told him about getting saved because of old Annie Chizim.

Bill looked over at his uncle who was standing at the base of the hanging tree, in just his orange overalls – unzipped to the fly of his jeans – and an old *I'm with the BIG Guy* T-shirt that had an arrow pointing towards his belt line. Ziggy was fiddling with the knotted rope that held the deer suspended in the air.

He lifted his shaggy head, blew at the haggard whiskers of his mustache, and looked over at Bill. "You'll get a banana in your pocket too when you shoot your first female." He ginned, looped the rope one last time and pulled it tight.

"Not allowed guns at university," Bill said.

Ziggy looked up at him. "Not talkin about murder. What are you? A friggin psychopath?" He smiled, scratched his head and pulled out his hunting knife.

"You mean I should take out my frustrations vicariously?"

"Vica-what?"

"Nothing."

Bill watched Ziggy approach the dangling carcass, bow to it cordially and then grab its snout and slit its throat. "Bet you wanna do that to that friggin girl, eh?" Ziggy chuckled as he wiped his knife blade.

Bill licked his chapped lips and winced a little when he ran his tongue over the canker in his mouth. He grabbed his one fist in the other and breathed warm air into his hands. "I'm over the criticism thing," he said to Ziggy as his uncle walked past him, wiping bloody hands on a gas-soaked rag.

"What?"

"You can drop the girl. I'm over it."

Ziggy looked him in the eye and Bill could tell he'd offended his uncle who'd only been going on about the girl in his class because he was trying to make his nephew feel better. Ziggy turned and looked at the doe's body slowly spinning in the late afternoon air that was alive with snow dust falling from tree boughs; blood dripped slowly in thick coagulated drops from the deer's nose. "Enjoy the friggin mobile," Ziggy said to Bill as he walked past him towards the door of the cabin.

He stopped at the door and looked back over his shoulder at Bill. "Can't cut her down once you've strung her up." Then he went inside and closed the door.

Bill shivered. He looked at the dead deer spinning slowly in the grey air. Stomped his feet in his heavy Kodiak boots. And blew into his frozen fingers, fisted as if in prayer.

PJ, wiry and young-looking for his forty years, was up by 4:30 am and out feeding the hounds. His son, Duncan, had gotten up with him and was polishing his dad's .308 when Bill climbed down out of the loft after his uncle.

"Where's Dan?" Ziggy asked Duncan groggily.

"Outside. Chopping wood or praying."

"Oh," Ziggy said and awkwardly crossed himself. He was what Dan would call a backslidden Catholic, like his friend Reg, but he preferred to think of himself as indigenously unhypocritical, though it was Bill and not Ziggy himself who would have worded it that way.

"You doggin with your dad today?" Bill asked Duncan.

"Nope. He's putting me on my own watch."

Ziggy went over and put a pot of water to boil on the propane stove. "You take one of them hunter safety courses at high school?"

"Yup. Got my license this year. And a tag. Dad gave me his old 30/30."

"Cool," Bill said as he turned and walked over to the hearth to retrieve his boots.

Ziggy stood at the stove and stared into the pot of water.

"Watched pot don't boil," Bill said as he walked past his uncle and sat at the table to lace up his boots.

"No shit, Sherlock," Ziggy muttered.

"Eh?"

"How long you in for?"

"Till tomorrow night."

"Three days?" Ziggy asked as he took a fistful of coffee grounds from the Folger's can and dropped them in the water that had just begun to boil.

"Yup," Bill quipped from where he was sitting at the table on a tin chair, tying up his big boots.

"Then back to school, eh?" Ziggy stirred the grounds into the water with a wooden spoon, put a lid on the pot, turned off the stove and went over to the hearth at the other end of the cabin to get his own boots.

"Yup. Then back to the city."

"Got to have another story for that writing class of yours?"

"Yeah, I do." Bill double-knotted his last bootlace and sat up.

Duncan put on his heavy orange coat, took his dad's .308 in one hand, pulled down his 30/30 from the gun rack behind the door, and then headed outside, letting in a cold draft.

Bill walked behind Dan and his uncle Ziggy through the woods, thinking of different ways he'd tried to describe the forest in his stories. Depictions of the bush all sounded alike in all the books he'd ever read that were set in the wilderness – a unique sameness in bushlands.

No wonder the ancient Celts believed forests were mystical portholes to an otherworld, he thought as he stepped in his uncle's tracks — Dan's being too irregular in spacing because of the older man's bad hip.

Silence, symphonic and whole, played in the spaces between footfalls. The crunch of snow underfoot syncopated their march up a ridge called The Suicide. Ziggy's cheeks were red when they reached the top; Dan was wheezing a bit but stood with a straight back despite the eighty-five years of living that weighed on his shoulders like a yoke.

Bill looked at his uncle and the old deacon from the Pentecostal church as he raised the shotgun he'd been carrying, crooked over his arm, to hold it in both gloved hands. "Where to, oh wise and aged ones?"

Dan's smile wrinkled his face beneath his thick glasses. Ziggy arched a wild eyebrow, snorted and said, "You bring shit tags?"

Bill looked at his uncle blankly. "What?"

"T.P.?"

"Eh?"

"Toilet paper," Dan said.

"You got any?" Ziggy asked again.

"No. Why?"

"Guess you don't need any, eh? When you got a diaper on."

It took two seconds for it to sink in but eventually Bill got it and he just shook his head because he couldn't think of a good retort. "So which way you want me?" he asked, humbled.

"See that squat of bushes down in the ravine there. That's your foxhole, Rambo."

"Where are you setting up?"

"I'm going up the far ridge on the other side and Dan's going to stay here. Hopefully PJ and Duncan will hound the deer straight down the ravine."

"So you two will be shooting directly at me?"

"Your mom hold her breath for nine months?"

"What?"

"Dan's going further up the ridge that way, ahead of where you'll be. And I'm going to be behind you facing the other direction. Dan and me will shoot only in the direction we're facing and you can shoot wherever you want as long as it isn't above your head. But you shouldn't have to worry about that unless a deer decides to leapfrog you."

"So," Bill breathed as he ran his tongue over the canker in his mouth, "when you don't have me who do you usually send into No Man's Land?"

Ziggy glanced up at Dan who was staring at his boots. "Dillan Witaker."

"Harold's dad?"

"Yeah." The silence was a cup of saliva they all tried to swallow without gagging. "That kid almost drowned once, in the swamps cause of a thaw."

"Harold's dad don't come out no more, eh?"

"Not since his boy overdosed and killed that professor guy."

"Sometimes," Dan said quietly, "sometimes prodigals come home."

Ziggy looked up at Dan's wrinkled face. "I respect the hell out of you, Dan," he said, "but Harold isn't coming home and no Sunday school Bible story's going to change that."

"God's still—"

"On hold!"

Ziggy and Dan stared at each other until Bill felt he should turn away from the tableau. It looked for a second as if Dan was going to say something but he snapped his mouth shut, turned and starting walking away towards his watch.

Dan's movement was like ice breaking under Bill's feet: he suddenly felt submerged in the early morning cold.

"Show yourself then," Bill heard his uncle mutter. Ziggy looked up at Bill, his seaweed green eyes iced over with cold memories. "If Mary would quit coddlin Jesus he might have half a second to set things straight down here."

And with that he headed down the ridge into the ravine, his 30/30 slung over his shoulder, his head down, eyes on his boots scuffing in the ankle-deep snow. Bill watched his uncle's wiry figure dust down the hill. He opened his mouth and swallowed a breath of winter air that lodged in his throat like an ice cube.

"Thought Dan said you were a crack shot," Bill said, peeling a potato beside Ziggy that night at the hunting camp, after the day had been called short because fifteen shots were fired and no deer bagged. PJ suggested the trigger-happy ones – Bill and Ziggy – make an early dinner so they could all head to bed before ten o'clock and sleep off any jitters.

Ziggy glared up at Bill. "I kid you not, there were four deer doing a friggin dance around me up on that ridge."

"Doesn't that make it worse though?"

"Eh?"

"There were four. Shouldn't you have at least got one?"

"Least I wasn't making no friggin snow angels on my watch!"

"That was after the shooting."

"Weren't you the first to fire?"

"Yeah, but your friggin shotgun kicked back and I lost my footing. Fell into my own turd pile."

"It's got a helluva kick but not enough to knock a man off his feet."

"Maybe back in the sixties when you last used it. You ever clean the thing?"

"Am *I* using it?"

"So you never—"

"Thought we said no women in the camp," Dan interrupted from the table behind them, his tin chair squeaking as he shifted his weight.

Ziggy whipped around, hair wild and wiry as steel wool on his scalp. Bill looked over his shoulder at Dan who was playing solitaire with the camp cards.

"Women?" Ziggy snapped.

"Thought we decided women was bad luck," Dan said slowly, looking for a place for an eight of spades.

"They are. Your point?"

"Yous are bickering like old women." Dan laid his card and flipped two more.

Jack of clubs.

Bill looked over his shoulder at his uncle trying to stare Dan down. He suddenly remembered the story he'd written about Dick and Vicky, his grandparents, and one of their fights in their cottage up on Lemming's Lake, and he wondered if a frying pan might go through a window here. Duncan was cleaning his 30/30 over by the fire. PJ was reading a ratty old paperback novel by John Irving.

"A woman couldn't have shot the only deer we got so far," Ziggy said.

"How many shots you take today?" Dan asked mildly, calculating his next move.

"Eh?"

"How many shots? Today."

"Ten."

"And?" Dan laid the jack of clubs and looked up. "Nothing. Right? Anne DeVries killed a black bear with one shot from a .22. Right through the eye."

"Bullshit."

"Ask John himself. Bear was in the garden and she got irate and shot it."

"So you saying Anne DeVries should hunt with us?"

"No."

"No, eh?"

"Just that if we're not letting the likes of Anne DeVries in on the hunt then why are we letting a whining old housewife like yourself in?" Dan looked to his cards, flipped two more.

Ace of diamonds.

"Outside," Ziggy said, putting his peeling knife down.

"What?" Dan asked, not looking up from the piles of cards on the table.

"Outside. You and me. Right now."

Dan looked up and smiled kindly, the skin around his eyes creased with old wrinkles. "Why?"

"You mock a guy's manhood and you can talk to his fist rather than his face. And don't use Jesus as an excuse to back down this time."

Dan looked sadly at Ziggy but he stood to his feet, stepped out from behind the table and lifted the latch of the door. "You comin?" he asked Ziggy without turning around.

"Right behind you," Ziggy huffed as he sucked in air to puff out his chest. The hairs of his mustache bristled. He walked past Bill and out the door behind Dan, fists clenched.

Bill blinked when the door slammed. He looked over at Duncan who was staring back at him, the oil rag in the kid's hand motionless. PJ flipped a page in his John Irving novel. Bill squinted to read the title: *The Cider House Rules*.

"Good book?" Bill asked.

"He's no Hemingway but it's all right."

Bill knew PJ was an avid reader: an independent academic, he'd called him in one of his stories. He heard a crash outside, over by the woodshed. "Should we—"

"Nope." PJ flipped another page, not lifting his eyes from the novel, his back against the log wall, his wool-socked feet up on the cot by the hearth.

Just as Bill was about to spin around and look out the window the door burst open and Ziggy stomped in with his head down. Bill could see blood on his uncle's mustache. Ziggy marched to the ladder of the loft and climbed quickly up it. An awkward silence stood in the room like a gangly kid.

Dan walked into the cabin, stepped behind the table and

sat down again with his cards. He flipped two more.

Three of diamonds.

He looked up at Bill, who stood with his back to the sink. Bill could tell Dan felt ashamed because his eyes dropped tiredly back to his cards and his shoulders slumped as if he was a really old man in a wheelchair.

Guess blood don't always bring peace, Bill thought as he turned back to the sink and continued to peel potatoes for his last supper in at the hunting camp.

In the morning Bill saw that Ziggy had a black eye and a swollen nose. "You okay," he asked his uncle after Duncan had climbed down out of the loft.

"Yeah. Why?"

"Uhh ... well ... you got a black eye."

"Yup. Got a branch in the face last night. Out taking a pee." Ziggy stared at his nephew as he pulled his Dickie work pants over his skinny legs.

Bill knew his uncle knew *he* knew better, but that wasn't the point: so he dropped it along with his stare and rummaged around in his bag for a clean shirt and an extra sweater. Then he climbed down the ladder after Ziggy, who went straight to the stove to make coffee.

Duncan was sitting at the table counting out shells.

"Where's your dad?" Ziggy asked.

"Feeding the dogs."

"And Dan?"

"Praying out in the woodshed."

Bill smiled at this early morning ceremony that started

each day for his uncle and the boy. He watched his uncle look out the window towards the woodshed, slowly cross himself, and then — surreptitiously — raise his middle finger, grin crookedly, and then go about making the coffee.

"You run into a branch last night, Ziggy?" Duncan asked, not looking up from shell-counting but smiling to himself.

Ziggy turned around, leaned against the counter and licked his front teeth. "Your tiny dick fit in the barrel of that gun?"

Duncan's eyes snapped up, his smile momentarily gone. But then he laughed and said, "No. Use your toque for that business."

"Pulling the pud, eh? That'll make you go blind." Ziggy laughed and turned back to his coffee-making. "O, sweet glaucoma." Soon the aroma of fresh coffee haunted the cabin like a ghost and Bill found he had to step outside before the earthy smell brought tears to his eyes. God, I miss Harold, he thought suddenly, not knowing why. The presence of the potent aroma made him more painfully aware of the absence of Harold's fiddle music in the quiet of the cabin at night.

"Red sky this morning," Dan said as he limped up to Bill.

"Sailor take warning," Bill breathed, trying to swallow the lump that was stuck like a fishbone in his throat.

"Used to call a red sun rising like that a Baptism of Blood; meant the day would be hell most likely. Yup. But storms are good for something."

"What?"

"Gives the Master something to calm."

Bill thought of Jim Carrol and how he'd drowned in Lemming's Lake because a storm overturned his fishing boat; he thought of his friend Christopher, who'd been in the boat with Jim. Why hadn't God calmed that storm? Bill looked up into Dan's eyes, magnified behind the old man's thick glasses. Part of him wanted to make one of his uncle's smart-ass quips: to tell Dan not to be so religious. But Dan was who he was. And there was no changing him.

The older man limped past Bill and into the cabin. Bill heard him ask Ziggy what happened to his eye. "Yanking the lizard last night and my hand slipped," Ziggy quipped.

"Lizard?" Duncan laughed. "Salamander is more like it."

"You measuring my dragon while I was asleep?"

Bill heard the three of them in the cabin all laugh. And then Duncan came out the door with his 30/30 in one hand and his father's .308 in the other. Bill watched the boy round the edge of the cabin and head to the dog kennels. He heard the baying of the hounds as the sun hit the dirty window of the cabin, causing it to glow dark red like a bloodshot eye.

"You want the balsam bush again?" Ziggy asked Bill as they stood on The Suicide overlooking the ravine. Ziggy's eye was swollen shut but he didn't mention it.

"Yeah, I'll take the foxhole again if you want."

"Sure."

"Duncan taking Dan's spot?"

"No, Duncan's setting up at the opening of the ravine, near the swamp."

"He okay on his own?"

"Sure. Young lad's got to learn sometime. Who knows, he might even bag his first big buck before you."

"Probably, seeing as how he's PJ's son."

Ziggy laughed and spit, then clapped his nephew on the shoulder and started down into the ravine.

"Hey," Bill called after him.

"What?"

"Why'd you quit the church?"

"Why you asking?"

"Just came to me."

"Well, it just came to me to quit it, I guess. Never had a prayer answered in my whole damn life."

"That why Dan gets to you sometimes?"

"Yeah. Pisses me off that it's so easy for him. To believe."

"Well ..."

"No. No sermons for me. I'll have to see it to believe it. Speaking of seeing it though – keep your eyes peeled for that 20-point buck I missed yesterday. He's a trophy."

With that, Ziggy scuffed off down the hill into an empty world. Before Bill began his descent he looked in the direction of Dan's watch; he could see the sleeve of an orange coat like a flame hidden partway behind a large white pine. A big work-swollen hand – bare to the cold – gripped the barrel of a gun.

The snow began coming down around 10:30 am. Bill stood in his spot by the balsam bush. Occasionally a wind would come up the ravine and make the hair on his neck stand on end. He zipped the collar of his coat right up to his chin but the chill was already inside him, like how Dan described the infilling of the Holy Ghost, making his hands twitch and his knees shake.

The air was silent about him save for the skeletal scraping of branches against each other. Bill stamped his feet and wiggled his toes in his wool socks, trying to work the cold ache of near-frostbite out of his boots. He opened and closed his gloved hand on the double barrel of the shotgun.

The loudest thing in his hearing was his own heavy breathing. He sucked in a mouthful of cold air that made his teeth ache, and held it in his lungs till it hurt his chest and made him lightheaded. He'd held his breath like that when his classmates had sat around "critiquing" his story about Harold. But it really happened, he'd whispered. What works in reality doesn't always work in fiction, the girl had shot back, thinking she was doing him a favour by being so urbanely honest.

The cold air stung his eyes and made them water. He blinked and could feel the winter-air tears freeze to his eyelashes. He reached up with his trigger hand and rubbed his eyes, thinking of his friend Wes, who had plucked out his eyelashes after his brother Sean died trying to save their dog that had been doused in gas and set on fire by some neighbourhood bullies. Wes had told Bill the doctor said it was because of nerves.

Bill stood there in the falling snow, his mind following the ghost of this recollection of Wes into another memory: another story. As Bill stared straight in front of him to where the ridge walls of the ravine became steeper and narrower and curved away to the east and snow whirled around like ash, he recalled the big bonfire held behind Garret's house, up on the Ridge Road, when they burned the old dead tree that Garret had hung himself in last winter. Bill had just stood there as hot ash had landed on his nylon jacket and burned holes through the fabric, singeing his skin.

His skin felt like it was burning now in the cold early-November air.

A shot slapped the silence like a hot hand against a frozen cheek! Bill snapped out of his memories, feeling as if someone had just doused him with a bucket of icy water. Who was that? There was no sound of the hounds. The ensuing silence tasted like cotton balls in his mouth.

He took a step forward and then stopped, not wanting to walk into Dan's range of fire. He waited. Count to ten, he thought and then asked himself: Why are you panicking?

He heard movement up on The Suicide: Dan moving from his watch.

Bill headed up the ridge and fell in behind Dan, following his tracks through the bush along the narrow path of The Suicide toward the mouth of the ravine. His heart was punching the inside of his rib cage as he started to run, not fully knowing why. Then he heard a double shot from behind him: Ziggy calling for a regroup. He slowed, then turned and got lashed across the eyes by a poplar branch.

He cursed as he dropped his gun, squinted and rubbed his eyes with his gloved hands. He stopped when he heard another double shot from in front of him: in Dan's direction. He opened his eyes and could barely see through the tears that blurred his vision, making him think he was looking at the forest from under water.

It took a second for his vision to clear and for everything to come back into focus and then he was off again, following Dan's tracks along the narrow ridge towards Duncan's watch.

As he came to the end of the ridge, where the ground sloped down into the ravine and was covered in loose rocks beneath the powdery snow, he saw Dan kneeling beside Duncan's body: the boy's head exploded and blood splattered everywhere on the snow.

The wind came up and impaled Bill through the mouth as he took a sharp breath.

For a second he felt as if the temperature had dropped so low reality itself had frozen still. He heard no sound of trees and didn't move, until Dan bent beside the boy's body. Then he ran down the hill, falling and sliding on loose, snow-slicked stones.

The hounds! Their howls filled up the empty pockets of the wind. And then they were there: around Dan. Licking at Duncan's blood and whimpering.

"Git!" Dan roared, slapping a black hound in the snout. The sound of footfalls crunching through the snow drummed the air.

"What the fu—"

"Duncan!"

PJ pushed Dan aside and laid his bare hands on his son's chest. Bill heard Ziggy's short breaths over his shoulder. Ziggy's voice, quiet: "Is he ..."

Silence, like being buried alive, caved in on them.

"Is he breathing?" Ziggy whispered.

PJ looked up, eyes iced with tears. He looked around, as

if searching for a giant rewind button or something as useless as a band-aid, a fucking stretcher: anything.

But there was nothing, nothing but blood on the snow ... and pieces of skin. PJ hung his head; sobs caught in his throat and made him gag. Dan scooped up the bloody snow in his hands — big, red work-swollen hands — and began squeezing the snow into a ball.

Bill looked at him as if to say: What the hell are you doing?

But Dan didn't look up: only continued to pack the bloody snowball that stained his big frost-swollen hands, the skin broken and bleeding in the cold — the old man's blood mingling with the boy's.

PJ's body shook as he wailed silently, choking on his own tears. He didn't see Dan reach over Duncan's still body with the bloody snowball. He didn't see what Bill saw: Dan pressing the ball of bloody snow against the exploded side of Duncan's face.

But his hands felt Duncan's chest swell with a sudden gasp as Dan pressed the wad of snow to the boy's mangled head and whispered a strange word: "Shekinah."

Bill sat in his car in rush-hour traffic, somewhere on the 401 between Bayview and Yonge, on his way back to university, thinking about how the doctors had said Duncan had probably fallen asleep and fallen forward on his gun, setting it off. The bullet went into his mouth, tore through the cheek and up along the side of the face, just missing Duncan's right eyeball. The doctors said — when Bill told them how still Duncan's body had been when they found him — that his body was probably frozen in shock and that the snow to the face would have snapped him out of that.

But what of the bleeding that suddenly stopped?

The low temperature. The open veins cauterized in the cold.

It's all explainable, they had said after they had done major surgical procedures on Duncan's face: grafting skin from his tongue to the hole in the top of his mouth, sewing his cheek shut, taking skin from his buttocks to patch up what had been torn from his face.

But Bill remembered watching his uncle Ziggy chug a 750-milliliter bottle of Canadian Club whisky – in at the hunting camp after the ambulance had taken Duncan's breathing body away – and he remembered the feeling of drunkenness that had surged through his own veins, knowing the sensation came from a different source, and that Dan's three-syllabled utterance over Duncan's still body had pulled the stopper from that invisible bottle.

Shekinah. The Lord camps with us. In this ramshackle tabernacle of flesh.

The thought of this made him feel submerged like that day Dan held him under in Lemming's Lake to baptize him; the still air of the car all around him was like water to breathe. "I'm going under but he won't let me up," Bill whispered as he checked to change lanes. But the *he* in his utterance wasn't Dan.

Bill held the doctors' opinions and his own convictions in his mouth like a shot of Bailey's and a shot of lemon cordial: the curdled contents of this Cement Mixer shooter tasting bitter to him instead of sweet.

How in hell am I supposed to write this? he wondered as he flipped his visor down to keep the sun out of his eyes. He eased off the brake and the car inched forward. He swallowed and let out a breath, that strange word filling his mouth — *shekinah* — the *k* in the middle of the word a cut across his tongue: the lacerating certainty of a miracle.

ACKNOWLEDGEMENTS

While those who live there will undoubtedly know the true names of the places in this work and be able to recognize echoes of true stories, this remains a work of fiction in its entirety. To those who have never heard of St. Lola or St. Olga and wonder where these villages might fall on a map of northeastern Ontario, head north on Highway 62 from Belleville toward Bancroft – you'll pass it along the way, just don't expect there to be a sign.

I would like to thank Hugh Cook, who saw the genesis of this collection; David Adams Richards, for feedback on the stories, encouragement, friendship and coffee; John Terpstra and Jessica Grant for kind words; Rosemary Sullivan and the Creative Writing gang at the University of Toronto – Laura Boudreau, Jessica Druker, Joseph Frank, Helen Guri, Daniel Tysdal, and Naya Vandellon; Dan Postma, copy-editor extraordinaire; Joel Harsevoort, for setting me straight on classical music and narcotic use; Alex King for the photo; Mike Minor for his music; and all of the people at Breakwater for their enthusiasm, hard work and brilliance – Annamarie Beckel, Anna Kate MacDonald, Rhonda Molloy, Chad Pelley, Jackie Pope, and Rebecca Rose.

A special thanks to my parents, Ed and Irene, for love and support and prayers. And to Samantha, my wife, seer of light in dark places.

PHOTO BY ALEX KING (2009)

SAMUEL THOMAS MARTIN is from Gilmour, Ontario. He received an MA in Creative Writing from the University of Toronto. He enjoys hiking, canoeing and exploring his new home in St. John's, Newfoundland, where he lives with his wife Samantha and their dog Vader.